Flying Blind

THE COOPER KIDS ADVENTURE SERIES®

Flying Blind
The Legend of Annie Murphy
The Deadly Curse of Toco-Rey
The Secret of the Desert Stone

(Available from Crossway Books)

Trapped at the Bottom of the Sea
The Tombs of Anak
Escape from the Island of Aquarius
The Door in the Dragon's Throat

**Look for more books to come in the Cooper
Kids Adventure Series® from Tommy Nelson™.**

The Cooper Kids Adventure Series®

Flying Blind

Frank E. Peretti

Thomas Nelson, Inc.

Nashville

FLYING BLIND
Copyright © 1997 by Frank E. Peretti

Unless otherwise indicated, Scripture quotations are from the
International Children's Bible, New Century Version,
copyright © 1986, 1988.

Executive Editor: Laura Minchew
Managing Editor: Beverly Phillips

Library of Congress Cataloging-in-Publication Data

Peretti, Frank E.
  Flying blind / Frank E. Peretti.
    p. cm. — (The Cooper Kids Adventure Series® ; 8)
  Summary: When the small plane which his uncle allows him to
fly tumbles out of control, fourteen-year-old Jay relies on God's
help to land the aircraft safely.
  ISBN 0–8499–3646–2
  [1. Aircraft accidents—Fiction. 2. Survival—Fiction.
3. Christian life—Fiction.] I. Title. II. Series: Peretti, Frank E.
The Cooper Kids Adventure Series® ; bk. 8.
PZ7.P4254F1   1997
[Fic]—dc21   97–24275
                                           CIP
                                           AC

Printed in the United States of America

97 98 99 00 RRD 9 8 7 6 5 4 3 2 1

ONE

Jay Cooper sat in the 182 Skylane's right seat, his hand on the control yoke, watching the horizon over the plane's nose and enjoying the view of the Cascade Mountains passing below. A gentle wind from the Pacific Ocean was rippling over the snow-frosted peaks like river water over smooth stones, making the airplane's wings rock lazily and its nose nod and wag in little yeses and nos. With gentle corrections to the control yoke, Jay held the plane on course and maintained a steady descent rate of five hundred feet per minute. At fourteen, he was three years too young to be a licensed pilot. But he'd flown often enough with his father to know how to handle an airplane. When he turned seventeen, he would get his license. His mind was made up on that. For now, his Uncle Rex was sitting in the left seat as pilot-in-command, letting him take the controls for a while.

It was supposed to be a pleasure trip. The Coopers were in Seattle visiting Dr. Cooper's sister, Joyce, and her husband, Rex. Rex thought the kids might like to "take the plane up" for the afternoon.

Of course, it was just an excuse to fly—a pilot is always looking for one. Jay's sister, Lila, passed. Jay leaped at the chance.

It was supposed to be a pleasure trip, just a scenic flight around Mount Rainier to take pictures, then a leisurely return to Boeing Field in Seattle. It would be a chance for Rex to get in some flight time and for Jay to gain a little more flight experience.

And it *was* a nice trip—for the first hour and ten minutes.

They'd circled Mt. Rainier, snapped some spectacular pictures, then practiced some maneuvers for Jay's benefit. When clouds began to build around the mountaintops, they decided it was time to turn for home and start the descent toward Seattle.

Skylane N758YT—the N was always pronounced "November," the Y and T were always pronounced "Yankee Tango"—had that typical Cessna light plane shape familiar to almost anyone near any airport in America. Its wings were on top of the airplane's body or fuselage, its two main wheels were on thin, springy legs sticking out just under the cabin, its one front wheel was under the nose, and it had one engine and propeller up front.

It had room for four people and several suitcases and was painted white with racy red stripes on the sides and wings.

And like most small, single-engine airplanes, "The Yank," as Uncle Rex liked to call it, was noisy inside. The 230-horsepower engine was spinning the propeller at more than 2,000 revolutions per minute while a 140-knot wind rushed over the airplane's aluminum skin, creating a roar like the ocean. So as Jay and Rex flew, they chatted with each other through their headsets, speaking into the tiny black microphones in front of their mouths and listening to each other through the big noise-deadening earphones. Without the headsets they would have to yell to be heard.

"I first flew in the service," Rex was explaining. "Got it in my blood and had to keep it up after I got out. The thrill isn't exactly the same, but it'll do. Yes sir, it'll do."

Jay smiled. Rex was a large, bearded man, who weighed about 230 pounds and all of it was muscle. He'd flown fighter jets in the Air Force and often told tales of tight maneuvers, aerobatics, G-forces, and throwing up. His flying stories always made Lila cringe, but Jay thought it was great stuff.

"My Dad learned while he was going to college," Jay replied. "I guess he figured he'd need an airplane if he was going to go out on archaeological digs."

"His is a 182, right?"

"Yeah, a lot like this one, only his is a little older and a little beat-up. It's been a lot of places, and some of the places weren't very nice."

Rex raised his eyebrows. "Oh, he's told me about some of the places you've been, how you've been stranded, shot at, chased, captured. I don't think I'd want that kind of work."

Jay shrugged. "Aw, you need a little excitement once in a while."

Rex laughed. "Yeah, roger that."

They had descended to four thousand feet. Below

them, logging operations had scarred the Cascade foothills like hundreds of bad haircuts; gray highways with ant-sized vehicles wound through the valleys; brown logging roads wriggled like snakes up the contours of the mountain slopes. Twenty-five miles to the northwest, the city of Seattle stretched out like a layer of coarse gravel on green felt. Beyond that, Puget Sound shimmered blue and glassy smooth, and beyond that, the Olympic Mountains formed a majestic, sawtoothed horizon.

"Woo!" Jay exclaimed. "Those mountains are looking good!"

Rex nodded. "Much better weather to the west. I'm glad we're going that way."

At that very moment, at Seattle-Tacoma International Airport just south of Seattle, a WestAir Boeing 757 had finished boarding passengers, and a flight attendant was sealing up the big cabin door. On the flight deck, Captain Jess Crylor was going through the engine start-up checklist as the two big jet engines came to life with their deafening whine.

"Seattle Ground," he radioed the tower, "WestAir 271 ready for push back." He was talking to the man in the tower who directed airplane traffic on the ground.

"WestAir 271, Seattle Ground," came the reply from the tower. "You are clear for push back, follow the Northwest 727 to 16 Left."

The ground controller was giving him permission to push back from the gate and telling him to follow another airliner, a Northwest Airlines 727, that was already on the taxiway. Runways at airports are numbered according to the direction they are pointing in compass degrees, leaving off the last zero. North on a compass is 360 degrees, so a runway pointing straight north would be called Runway 36. South on a compass is 180 degrees, so a runway facing south would be called Runway 18. Seattle-Tacoma has two runways side by side, situated at 160 degrees, called 16 Left and 16 Right. Both airliners would be taxiing to runway 16 Left for takeoff.

Captain Crylor radioed back, "WestAir 271." Every time a pilot receives instructions from a control tower he or she responds by saying the number of the aircraft. That way, the controllers can be sure the right person received the right instructions.

There was a slight bump as the powerful ramp tractor hitched onto the 757's nose gear and started pushing the airliner back from the gate.

In the cabin, the flight attendants got out their demonstration seat belts and oxygen masks in preparation for the safety instruction routine. "Good afternoon, ladies and gentlemen. If you'll direct your attention to the flight attendant standing at the front of the cabin, we will go over the safety features of our Boeing 757 aircraft. To be sure your seatbelt is fastened. . . ."

On the flight deck, Captain Crylor and his copilot were reading off checklists, twisting knobs, and flipping switches, checking out all the aircraft's systems. Everything was checking out okay. They were expecting a routine flight to Salt Lake City.

And it would be a routine flight . . . for the first thirty seconds.

Rex and Jay were approaching Seattle's outskirts, dropping down to fifteen hundred feet. Rex took the controls of The Yank and set his radios.

"We're going by the Auburn airport. Think I'll tune them in and see if there are any other planes flying around I should know about." Then he perked up with an idea. "Listen, we have to come into Boeing Field from the north. How about we swing around north and take a quick tour of downtown Seattle?"

Jay nodded happily. "Sounds good."

"Great. Well, we'll just hang a left here."

Rex turned The Yank to the left and set a course that would pass a few miles south of Seattle-Tacoma International. He was careful to keep the airplane at fifteen hundred feet, a legal and safe altitude that would keep him down low, out of the way of the big jets departing from that airport.

WestAir 271 taxied into position on runway 16 Left and immediately received clearance from the tower, "WestAir 271, you are clear for takeoff."

Captain Crylor gave the throttles a firm, even

advance, the engines' whine rose to a roar, and the big bird began to speed down the runway.

Just then, Rex and Jay heard a voice through their headsets. "Auburn traffic, Piper Cub eight eight niner on forty-five to right downwind, one six, Auburn."

Rex grinned as he radioed, "Hey Chuck, is that you?"

Chuck's voice came back, "That sounds like Rex Kramer. How you doin'?"

"Fine as frog's hair, buddy. Just took my nephew on a little trip around Mount Rainier."

"Good day for it."

"Take care."

"You too."

Rex told Jay, "That was Chuck Westmore. He flies a little Piper Cub out of Auburn Municipal." Suddenly he pointed. "Hey, there he is at two o'clock."

Jay knew that his uncle wasn't telling him what time it was, but what direction to look, based on the idea of a clock face. If you were to lay a huge clock down flat and then stand in the center of it facing the twelve, then twelve o'clock would be straight ahead, six o'clock would be straight behind you, three o'clock would be directly to the right, and nine o'clock directly to the left. Since Uncle Rex said two o'clock, Jay looked to his right and a little ahead, and sure enough, there was a small yellow airplane heading for its airport.

"The Cub's a nice little airplane," said Rex. "You could just about land it in your driveway."

In the short moment they were watching the Cub, Jay and his uncle did not notice the huge jet lifting off from Seattle-Tacoma. On their present course, they would be flying directly beneath the airliner's flight path. On any other day, under normal circumstances, the jet would be so high above them there would be no danger. But not today.

The WestAir 757 was heading skyward like a rocket, climbing through 500 feet, 1,000, 1,500. . . .

ALARMS! The plane shuddered. Red lights flashed on the instrument panel. The 757 lurched to the right.

Captain Crylor corrected with the control yoke and jammed on the left rudder pedal as he scanned the engine instruments and adjusted the throttles. "Loss of fuel pressure, right engine."

"Pump malfunction," the co-pilot shouted, his hands darting all over his control panel, "switching to auxiliary, manual override. . . ."

The airliner's right engine was winding down, losing power. With only the left engine running, the aircraft was slowing, shuddering, weaving crazily, and finally forced to the right. Crylor kept his foot on the left rudder pedal to hold a straight course. He pushed the yoke forward, lowering the nose to pick up some speed. It would cost him some altitude but he had to keep the airplane flying.

Chuck Westmore was purring lazily along in his Piper Cub, getting ready to land, when the huge jet caught his attention. He'd lived, worked, and flown near Seattle-Tacoma for years. He knew what the takeoff of a big jet was supposed to look like. When he saw the 757 wobbling and dropping instead of climbing, he immediately knew something was wrong.

He canceled his landing, applied power, and circled around to keep the jet in view. It was in trouble, all right. It was losing altitude, wobbling, and exhaust was coming from only one engine. The other must have malfunctioned. If the pilot didn't get control soon. . . .

Oh no! Chuck thought his heart would stop. Was that little white speck over there Rex Kramer's Skylane? The 757 was heading right for it!

Chuck fumbled for his handheld radio microphone. Was Rex still on the Auburn frequency?

"Rex! Can you hear me?"

Rex's voice came back, "Yeah, Chuck?"

Thank God! Chuck thought. "Heads up, Rex, there's a jet coming at you at three o'clock! He's low. He's really low."

Rex and Jay looked to the right in time to see a string of black jet exhaust trailing out of sight above their right wing. A shadow swept over them. They caught just a glimpse of a wingtip bigger than their whole airplane.

Quicker than their next thought, the horizon went crazy, the ground and sky traded places, and the walls and ceiling of the cockpit came at them with freight train force, bashing their skulls.

"NOOO!" Chuck screamed as he saw the Skylane flip over like a leaf in the wind, tumbling totally out of control. "Dear God, no! Rex! Rex! Can you hear me?"

On the flight deck of the 757, Captain Crylor and his co-pilot didn't see or feel a thing.

"Negative function, Cap," reported the co-pilot. "The right engine is out cold."

"Roger that," said Captain Crylor. He'd been trained to handle the loss of an engine on takeoff and had already made the necessary corrections. The big jet stabilized, flying on one engine. "Easy does it. We're low, but we're flying. We'll take her back around for an emergency landing."

The copilot noticed the rooftops not so far below. "We'll give the people in those houses a scare, I suppose." He radioed the Seattle-Tacoma tower. "Seattle Tower. Emergency. WestAir 271 has lost an engine."

Jay felt numb, dizzy, sleepy. No pain, no fear. Looking straight ahead through the windshield, the roofs of a suburban neighborhood seemed to be spinning, coming closer and closer. It wasn't real. It seemed more like a movie playing in front of his dazed eyes. Wow, he thought.

Then everything went black.

As Chuck watched in horror, the big jet continued on, climbing slowly, unaffected, like a big truck that has just run over a small animal and left it tumbling onto the road's shoulder. The 757 had not touched Rex Kramer's plane. It didn't have to. Just as the wake from a big ship can upset a canoe, so the terrible wake turbulence kicked up by such a monstrous aircraft can wash like a tidal wave over a light plane close behind and below it.

The Skylane was right side up again after flipping completely over, but now it was banked sharply to the left with the nose down, spiraling in a tight, corkscrew turn.

"Rex!" Chuck shouted. "Rex! Can you hear me? You're spiraling, Rex! You're going to crash! Rex, come in!"

No answer.

The plane just kept circling tightly, dropping lower and lower toward the rooftops.

TWO

Chuck flew closer and kept calling over the radio, "Rex! Rex! Please answer, can you hear me? Rex, you've got to pull up or you'll rotate into the ground! Rex, you hear me?" Then he silently prayed, Dear Lord, please wake him up, nudge him, get him on those controls!

Aboard the Skylane, Jay was asleep, dreaming about riding a merry-go-round and hearing somebody yelling for his Uncle Rex. Whoever it was just kept yelling and yelling and Jay started wondering, *Why doesn't Rex answer?*

Then he became aware of noises: the rush of wind, a loud engine revving and shaking, metallic vibrations and rattles getting louder and louder.

Jay felt sick, like he'd been on the merry-go-round too long.

"Rex!" There was that voice again. "Rex, please answer me!"

"Uncle Rex," Jay muttered, "somebody wants you. . . ."

"Rex!" came the voice through his headphones.

Jay's hand went to his ear and bumped into the large ear protector of his headset. It finally registered in his mind: *It's the radio! Somebody's calling us!*

"Level the wings, Rex! Get that nose up! Come on now!"

Jay's mind cleared enough to think, *Oh man. Something isn't right here. We're in trouble. What's happened?*

Fear stung him through the heart. The dream was over and he'd awakened to a nightmare. He groped for the control yoke, found it, and pulled back.

Oof! His body was pressed into the seat as if he weighed a ton. G-forces. Like in tight turns. The kind that make you want to barf.

"Level the wings, Rex!" came the voice.

Level the wings? What was wrong with the wings? He pressed his radio talk button and asked, "Uh, which way?"

"You're spiraling to the left, Rex! Roll out to the right!"

Jay cranked the yoke to the right.

Oof! G-forces again. *I'm going to barf, I just know it!*

Chuck saw the Skylane snap out of the turn and then swoop skyward like a barn swallow, climbing, slowing, climbing, slowing more, hanging from the propeller.

"Get the nose down, Rex! You're going to stall!"

14

Jay shoved the yoke forward. *Ooooohh,* he felt like his stomach was in his throat.

The plane went over the top of the climb and nosed down, going into the same sickening left spiral. Sweat was trickling down Chuck's face. He felt he was watching the death of Rex Kramer being played out before his very eyes. "Level the wings, Rex, you're spiraling!"

"Which way?" came a voice through Chuck's headphones.

Suddenly Chuck realized it wasn't Rex Kramer's voice. It must be Rex's nephew! "Level the wings, get the plane level!"

"Which way?" the nephew asked again.

"Right. Bank to the right—NOT TOO MUCH!"

The Skylane teetered to the right and swooped upward again the moment the wings were level.

"Full throttle! Ease the yoke forward, get the nose down!"

The Skylane went into a dive again. *No, no, no! Can't this kid see what he's doing?*

This was just like a ride on the world's biggest roller coaster, and Jay was getting sicker and sicker. His stomach was churning. He could feel that awful

15

tingling around his jaws that usually came just before the sudden loss of a meal. He drew in some deep breaths and rubbed his eyes with a free hand. If only he could *see!* Something kept blocking his vision— sweat, or blood, or his hair or something. All around him, The Yank's frame, skin, and engine were roaring, vibrating, screaming louder and louder.

"Pull back the power," came the voice through his headset. "You're going to overspeed!"

He reached out blindly, groping for the throttle knob somewhere down to his left. He found a knob and yanked it out as far as it would go.

The engine calmed, the noise settled.

On what was usually a quiet street in a neighborhood south of Seattle, a retired mailman and his wife were enjoying a lemonade in their backyard when they heard an aircraft engine come closer, closer, closer, and then suddenly quit, leaving only a rushing, windy sound.

The man rose from his lawn chair and looked up at the sky through the tops of his fruit trees.

WHOOOOSH! An airplane swooped so low over their yard the wind from its wings made the fruit trees tremble.

"Get the nose up! Ease it back slowly. . . ."

Jay pulled. He could feel himself pressed into his

seat again. The roller coaster was going up another hill.

The retired mailman fell to the ground, scared out of his wits. His wife screamed. The airplane just missed the roof of their house and soared upward into the sky again, the engine still quiet.

Jay tried to relax. He was overdoing everything and he knew it, torturing this airplane and his own body. He was climbing again, he was sure of it.

But it was strangely, frighteningly quiet. There was no sound but the wind rushing over the airplane's wings and skin, and now that was getting quieter too. He felt like he was slowing down.

"Okay," came the voice. "Add some power now and ease the nose down."

He reached for the throttle and this time found several knobs all side by side. Which one was the throttle? He pushed on one. Nothing happened.

What happened to the engine? Why isn't it running?

Quiet. Nothing but the wind outside.

"You're starting to drop again," came the voice. "Get that power in."

Jay felt a stab in his stomach. *The mixture! I've starved the engine!* His mind was a blank. He groped for the correct knob. He couldn't think.

"Which one is it?" he asked desperately.

"Just shove everything forward. *Everything!*"

He groped again, put the palm of his hand across all the knobs, and shoved them all in as far as they would go.

The engine came to life with a roar that surged through the whole airplane. He could feel the nose lurch skyward. That *was* what was happening, wasn't it?

He rubbed his eyes. He still couldn't see where he was going.

He could feel the airplane turning to the right. He turned the yoke left.

"Level those wings," came the voice. "You're going into a spiral again."

"Which way should I turn?" Jay asked.

Chuck answered, "To the right, just a little." The Skylane's left wing came up and it leveled out of the spiral. "That's it, that's it. Now hold the yoke neutral. Don't turn anymore."

"But I'm turning *now!*" the lad responded.

"No you aren't. I can see you from here and you're—" A thought hit Chuck like the world's worst news: Maybe this kid really *can't* see. "You're not turning. You only think you are."

"I'm turning!"

"Son, what's your name?"

"Jay Cooper." He sounded scared.

"Can you see out the window?"

"No. I can't see anything."

"Can you see the controls in front of you?"

"No."

Oh no. Oh no, Chuck thought. "Jay, are you blind?"

Jay rubbed his eyes again, blinked several times, and strained to see something, anything. Sometimes he could sense light coming through the windshield, but that was all. He felt his face again in case a sheet or hat or some other object was blocking his eyes. He found nothing in front of his face, but could feel something wet and sticky running down his forehead. It had to be blood.

"No, I'm not blind. I mean, not usually. I just can't see right now. I think I hit my head." He could hear Eight Yankee Tango roaring from nose to tail. He felt the airplane was going somewhere in a big, powerful hurry. "What's happening? What's the airplane doing?"

Oh Lord. He is *blind.* Now Chuck was scared but tried to speak in a calm voice. "Jay, right now you're climbing, and that's good, but you need to be careful to keep those wings level. I'll tell you how, all right? You hear me, Jay?"

"I hear you."

19

Chuck was maneuvering, trying to keep the Skylane in sight. He'd opened up his throttle for more speed, but the little Piper Cub was having trouble keeping up. He could feel his heart pounding and the blood pulsing through his fingers as he pressed the button on his microphone to speak. "All right, you're still climbing. You're starting to veer to the left again. Can you give it just a touch of right aileron?" *Does he know what* aileron *means?* "Uh, just a little tilt to the right?"

The airplane tilted back to level again, then past it into a right bank.

"That was a little too much. Give it a touch of left now."

The Skylane rolled back to almost level.

"Okay, that's good right there. But it won't stay there by itself. Can you find the throttle?"

Jay cringed. The last time he thought he was pulling back the throttle he'd pulled back the fuel mixture and killed the engine. "I . . . I think so. I just can't remember which one it is."

Chuck winced. He wasn't familiar with a 182 and couldn't be entirely sure himself. He'd flown some smaller Cessnas. He strained to remember, to see the control panel in his mind. "Um . . . let's try the second from the left. The first one with a bigger knob."

Jay reached down to his left and found the row of knobs again. There were four altogether, a small one on the left end and then three bigger ones. "Okay, I'm going to pull back on the second one."

"A little right aileron, Jay. You're starting to turn left again."

Jay gave the yoke a short little tweak to the right.

"Good. That's real good." The man's voice calmed a bit. "You must know what an aileron is."

"Sure. Ailerons are those little panels on the back edge of the wing that tilt up and down and make the airplane bank." Giving that little explanation helped calm Jay's nerves. Maybe that was why this guy in his headset brought up the subject.

"Okay, Jay, you get an *A* for the day." Jay had to smile at the silly rhyme. "Now let's try that throttle."

Jay could feel terror gripping him. "What if it's the wrong knob?"

"Just pull it slowly, just an inch or so, and listen to the engine."

He took hold of the knob and pulled it out slowly. He couldn't tell if it was making a difference or not.

"How's it going?" came the voice.

"I can't tell if anything's happening."

"Pull some more," Chuck said.

Jay pulled the knob out another inch. Now the engine seemed to calm a little. "I . . . I think it's the throttle. The engine's easing up a little."

"Pull just a little more."

Oh Lord, don't let it be the mixture knob! He pulled another inch. The engine quieted. He thought he felt a sinking feeling. "Am I diving again?"

"No, you're just starting to level off from your climb. You're doing good. Just leave the throttle there a moment. Right aileron again, just a touch."

Jay rested back in his seat and gave the yoke another tilt to the right. He told himself out loud, "All right Jay, now just be cool and pretend you're flying with Dad." Then he prayed, "And Lord, please help me. I'm in trouble."

"What happened to Rex?" came the voice.

Jay reached over with his left hand and could feel Rex sitting there, slumped over, his head bowed, not moving. "Uncle Rex? Uncle Rex, can you hear me?"

"Is he breathing?"

Jay's hand groped upward and found his uncle's jaw and mouth. He could feel warm breath coming from Rex's nose. "Yeah, he's breathing. But he must be unconscious. I'm poking him right now and he doesn't do anything."

"Jay, does that airplane have an autopilot?"

Now that would be nice! "I don't know. I've never been in this plane before."

"Give it a touch of right aileron."

Jay gave it a touch. "What happened?"

"A big 757 came right over the top of you and you got caught in its wake turbulence. It wasn't your fault. The jet wasn't supposed to be flying that low. It looked to me like it was having engine trouble. Aside from not being able to see, how are you?"

"I'm sick. I feel like I'm going to throw up, and . . ." Jay felt his head again. "My head's bleeding and it hurts like crazy."

"Give her some more right aileron, Jay."

Jay tilted the yoke to the right just a moment, then returned it to neutral.

Chuck could see the Skylane's wings level up again as it continued a gradual, slower climb. "Jay, you're doing terrific. Just keep giving it that much correction whenever I tell you. Just a touch, okay?"

"Okay. By the way, who are you and where are you?"

Chuck laughed. "Sorry for not introducing myself. I'm Chuck Westmore, a friend of your uncle's. I'm following you right now in my airplane."

"Are you the guy in the Piper Cub?"

"Yeah, that's right. Have you ever flown an airplane before?"

"Yeah, my Dad's airplane."

"Is it like your uncle's?"

"Pretty much. They both have a 182."

"That's great. Have you ever landed a plane?"

"Yeah, my Dad's."

Chuck felt a touch of relief, of hope. He knew they weren't out of the woods yet, but at least they had a fighting chance. "That's great, Jay. That'll sure help. Now let's work out a little code, all right? If I say left, you give it just a little bit of left aileron and then come back to neutral, okay? If I say right, then you do the same thing to the right. Same for up and down, you understand?"

"Yeah, all right."

"The biggest danger is overcorrecting, doing too much of something. We have to do it in small pieces, slow and easy." The Skylane was starting to veer to the right. "Okay, give it a touch of left."

Now the airplane rocked back to level again. Good. This kid was doing all right so far.

He had to call for help, but there was no time to do that and still talk to the lad to keep him flying safe and level. *Aviate, then navigate, then communicate,* went the old pilot safety slogan. *Oh well,* he thought, *one thing at a time. We'll wake 'em up with the transponder. At least they'll know where we are.*

On the right side of Chuck's control panel was a small black box with four numbers and a little knob under each number. This was his transponder. Every time a beam from a radar station would sweep over the plane, the transponder would send back a signal telling the people in the control tower the number or code on the transponder and the plane's altitude. Right now the four numbers were set to 1200, a code that meant he was just out buzzing around in clear weather. No doubt there were several airplanes in the area with transponders set to that same code, so the people in the control tower wouldn't be able to tell them apart. But that was about to change. He started twisting the knobs until the number was 7700, a universal distress code.

That should wake them up, he thought.

In the control tower at Boeing Field, the controllers had just heard about the WestAir 757 making a safe emergency landing at nearby Seattle-Tacoma International and were breathing a sigh of relief. They'd been on alert in case the 757 needed to land at Boeing, but now that whole mess was over, and they could get back to their regular routine. Ben Parker, the tower chief, a veteran air-traffic controller with a graying crew cut and somber expression, allowed himself at least a slight glint of happiness in his eyes. Apart from that he was silent, his hands on his hips, as he watched his staff of three men and two women cheer and give each other high fives.

Until the alarms went off. Loud beeps and blinking red lights on the control panels filled the room.

"We've got a seven-seven!" someone exclaimed. The cheering and talking stopped.

"Never a dull moment," Parker muttered, then called out, "All right, let's look alive, let's get on it!"

Every controller manned his or her station, monitoring the radios, searching the radar screens.

"Southeast," announced Barbara Maxwell, a dark-haired lady in her thirties wearing a small headset. "About fifteen miles out."

Ben Parker stared grimly over her shoulder. He could see the blinking target on her radar screen. "Any voice contact?"

Maxwell switched over to the universal emergency frequency and called, "Aircraft in distress, this is Boeing Tower. Come in." No answer. She repeated the call. Still no answer.

"They're near Auburn. They might be on the Auburn airport frequency," Parker thought out loud. "Bob, switch over to Auburn frequency. See if you pick up anything."

Bob Konishi, a youthful Asian-American, manned his radio panel, dialed in the frequency, and listened.

"We have two targets on the radar," Maxwell reported. "The seven-seven might be following another aircraft."

Konishi waved his hand. "I've got something!"

"Put it on the speaker," Parker said.

Konishi flipped a switch and the whole room could hear the voice of Chuck Westmore crackling from the overhead speaker: "You're doing real good, Jay. Now remember, when you can't see the ground outside, your body can lie to you. You can think you're turning when you aren't and think you're flying level when you're turning. You'll just have to ignore what your body is telling you and listen to me. Okay?"

"Okay," Jay's voice answered.

"Now stand by. I'm going to make a call and get some help. Just hang on."

Parker looked at Maxwell. She was monitoring the distress frequency. She would most likely get his message.

She nodded back. She was getting it, and switched it to the overhead speaker: "Mayday, Mayday, Piper Cub Eight Eight Niner in distress, anyone who hears me, please respond."

Maxwell replied through her headset, "November Eight Eight Niner, Boeing Tower, go ahead."

Chuck had two radios in his Cub. One was tuned to talk to Jay, the second was tuned to talk on the emergency frequency. It was on the second radio that Chuck got the response from Boeing Tower. He answered, "Eight eight niner about ten miles southeast of Auburn Municipal at two thousand five hundred feet. I'm following a Cessna Skylane. I'm in contact with the passenger. The pilot is unconscious. The passenger is conscious but blind."

The people in the tower were dumbfounded. Parker's eyes narrowed. "Say again," he prompted Maxwell.

"Say again," she told Chuck.

Chuck's voice came over the speaker, "The Skylane encountered wake turbulence from a low-flying 757. The pilot was knocked unconscious. His passenger, a young man, is conscious, but is injured and *he can't see.*"

"The WestAir 757," Parker muttered. He started barking out orders. "Bob, declare an emergency for November Eight Eight Niner, ground all aircraft leaving and redirect all aircraft arriving. Johnny, get the airport manager on the phone and tell him what we've got. We need the airport closed." Johnny

Adair, a plump man in his forties, grabbed up the telephone at his station. Parker quickly added, "And tell him we need emergency vehicles on stand-by." Adair nodded as he punched in the phone number. Parker went to his own station and put on his headset. "Eight Eight Niner, Seattle Tower. Does the Skylane have an autopilot?"

Chuck was straining to see the Skylane, still shrinking as it flew farther and farther ahead of him. "The passenger doesn't know."

"Do you know who owns the airplane?"

"Rex Kramer. He keeps it there at Boeing Field."

"*Where* at Boeing Field?"

"I'll have to ask the passenger if he knows. But listen, before the accident, Rex told me he'd just been out to Mount Rainier, so I'm sure he filed a flight plan."

Parker signaled Josie Fleming, a sharp-looking African-American controller who also worked as a flight instructor. She immediately started putting the information into a computer terminal as she heard it from Chuck.

"Can you give us a spelling on that last name?" Parker requested.

Chuck spelled it, Fleming tapped it out on the keyboard.

"Say the aircraft again."

"Cessna 182 Skylane. I don't know the tail number."

"Got it!" Fleming shouted as the flight plan for Rex Kramer and Skylane N758YT came up on the computer screen. "The plane is based at Jessup Aviation, right across the field from here."

Fleming was grabbing up a telephone even as Parker said, "We need to talk to someone familiar with that airplane: the guy's wife, his mechanic, anyone who can advise us on what equipment it has on board—and, does it have an autopilot?" He spoke into his headset again. "Eight Eight Niner, is the passenger flying the plane now?"

"That's affirmative. He's getting guidance from me, but he's getting too far away. I can hardly see him."

Parker stole a look at Maxwell, who glanced at her radar screen and nodded a confirmation. "The Skylane's pulling far ahead, about two miles now and increasing." Then she added quickly, "But there's another problem." Parker was there in an instant, viewing the radar screen over her shoulder as she pointed out the radar blip representing the Skylane. "Currently flying on a course of One-Zero-Five, altitude three thousand two hundred feet and climbing . . . but not climbing fast enough."

Parker nodded grimly, then spoke into the headset again. "Eight Eight Niner, how's the ceiling over those mountains?"

Chuck was dismayed as he observed, "Not good at all. The clouds are down over the mountaintops now."

"So the problem is that plane's either going to crash into those mountains or disappear into those clouds and *then* crash into the mountains. We have to get that plane turned around."

Chuck squinted into the distance. Sometimes he could see the wings of the Skylane like a tiny white dash against the gray slopes of the Cascades, and sometimes it would pass in front of the white clouds, making it hard for Chuck to be sure he was seeing anything at all.

"Jay," he called on his first radio, "Jay, come in."

"I hear you," Jay replied.

"Jay, we need—"

The Skylane was gone. A cloud, low and gray, and so much closer than Chuck had realized, had swallowed it up.

THREE

It's gone!" Chuck exclaimed over the radio. "It's gone into the clouds!"

Parker signaled to Maxwell and she took over, still watching the two blips on the radar screen. "Eight Eight Niner, confirm the Skylane is on 122.8."

Chuck responded, "That's affirmative. We're talking on the Auburn frequency."

Parker said quickly, quietly, "I'll take Eight Eight Niner, you take the Skylane." He spoke into his headset, "Eight Eight Niner, we have the Skylane on radar and we're getting an altitude readout from its transponder. We're going to try to turn it around. Please stand by, keep looking."

"Roger."

Maxwell asked Chuck, "What's the young man's name?"

"Jay Cooper."

"Stand by. I'm going to call him."

Parker flashed a quick look at Josie Fleming. She

was on the telephone that very moment. "I have the pilot's wife on the phone," she said.

Joyce Cooper Kramer, a pretty blonde in her forties, sat in her kitchen. To keep them from shaking, she had one hand clamped firmly on the phone, the other to the edge of the kitchen table. Her stomach was in a terrible knot and her mind was numbed with disbelief, but this was no time to be weak or frightened. Rex and Jay needed her. She took a deep breath to steady her voice and then replied to Fleming, "I believe the airplane does have an auto-pilot, but I don't know where it is or how it works."

"Is there anyone who would know?" Fleming asked.

"Call Brock Axley at Jessup Aviation, Boeing Field. He's Rex's mechanic. He knows that airplane."

"Brock Axley. Got it."

"But another thing."

"Yes?"

"The boy's father, my brother Jacob, is there at Jessup right now. He has a Skylane like Rex's. Please be sure he knows about this."

"Absolutely, Mrs. Kramer."

"I'm going to drive down to Jessup right now. If anything develops, *anything*, here's my mobile phone number. . . ."

"Ready to copy."

Joyce gave Josie Fleming her mobile phone number, hung up, and was out the door within one minute.

Jay had no idea he was in the clouds, which way he was going, or whether he was turning. He was beginning to wonder what had happened to Chuck. He hadn't heard from him in several minutes, but it seemed much longer. His life depended on a steady flow of words from his seeing-eye pilot. The silence was disheartening.

"Chuck? Are you there?"

"Jay," came Chuck's voice, "here's a lady from the Boeing Tower. Her name's Barbara and she's going to help you."

Barbara Maxwell was still watching the Skylane on radar as well as the brave little Piper Cub falling far behind. "Jay, this is Barbara. Can you hear me all right?"

"Yes ma'am."

Parker and the others were listening intently and exchanged concerned looks as they heard Jay's voice. This *was* just a kid!

"I'm watching you right now on radar. You're in a left turn, and that's good for right now. We want you to turn around. But your turn looks a little too steep. Can you give it a touch of right aileron?"

Jay answered, "Okay."

Parker and Maxwell watched the screen intently.

"Still too steep. He's starting to drop," said Maxwell. She spoke to Jay, "A little more right, Jay."

They waited to see if the motion of that little blip would change. The left turn seemed a little shallower, but they couldn't be sure.

Beads of sweat were forming on Maxwell's brow. "He's still dropping. He's down to two thousand five hundred."

"He's going to meet those mountains," Parker muttered. He called Chuck, "Eight Eight Niner, any contact?"

They could hear the fear in Chuck's voice as he replied, "Negative, he's still in the clouds."

Lila Cooper, thirteen, sat in the cockpit of a miniature P-51 Mustang and nervously gripped the control stick, imagining what it must be like to do a barrel-roll while sitting in that tight little space. The mini-Mustang was parked in a hangar at Jessup Aviation, its long nose jutting proudly and its big yellow propeller still and quiet. That being the case, Lila didn't mind trying out the pilot's seat and eyeing the instruments. Her slender frame fit the cockpit just fine, but if this plane was going to fly, she didn't want to be in it when it did. It was so small it was almost a toy.

"She'll do about two hundred ten knots," Brock Axley announced proudly, adjusting his billed cap on his frizzy gray head. "Fully aerobatic, with long-range tanks. I have taken her over to the Experimental Aircraft Fly-in twice." He and Lila's father, Dr. Jacob Cooper, were walking around the little airplane, admiring it from every angle. They'd lifted the cowling to study the engine, admired the flashy paint job, and talked the usual "hangar talk" about climb performance, stall speed, useful load and fuel endurance, and what little tricks the airplane could do.

Hmm, she thought. *Almost* a toy? No, it really *was* a toy. For two big kids standing in that hangar right now: the slightly chubby mechanic with the frizzy gray hair and her tall, handsome father. She smiled to herself.

"Yeah, nothing but fun," Brock said, patting the airplane on the nose as if it were a pup. "Next week we're going to try—"

The door to the office burst open and Nancy from the office stuck her head in. "Brock! Pick up line two, there's an emergency!"

Brock's mood immediately switched to serious. "Excuse me." He started toward the office.

"You too, Dr. Cooper!" Nancy shouted. "It's Rex and Jay! They're in trouble!"

Lila scrambled out of the cockpit, her heart racing.

Brock pointed to an extension phone on the wall of the hangar. "Take that one, Jake! I'll grab it in the office. Line Two."

Each man grabbed up a telephone and got the news at the same time. As Lila ran to her father's side, she could see the color drain from his face. "Where are they now?" he asked the person on the other end. "And no response from Rex?" He listened to the answer, then asked through the phone, "Brock, what about that autopilot?"

Lila could hear Brock's voice from the office, explaining something into the telephone.

Then Dr. Cooper said, "I know that airplane. I own a Cessna just like that Skylane! Jay's flown it. Brock has one here."

In the office, Brock agreed, "Yeah, practically the same model. I've serviced 'em both!"

Dr. Cooper listened a moment, scribbling some radio frequencies on his hand, then said, "We're on our way!" and hung up.

"Dad, what is it?" Lila cried.

Dr. Cooper's eyes were steely and intense. "That was the control tower. Jay and your uncle Rex have met some difficulty." Then he touched her shoulder and told her the situation as gently as he could.

She almost choked on the words, "What are we going to do?"

"Brock and I are going up in his 182 to chase Jay down and help him. The two airplanes are alike, with the same controls, the same performance speeds and power settings. We'll tell Jay how to make his airplane do whatever ours is doing and, I hope, bring him in."

"I've got to go with you!"

Nancy shouted again, "Dr. Cooper, it's your sister! She's calling from her car! She's on her way here."

Dr. Cooper grabbed the phone again. "Joyce. Yes, we just heard. We're taking off in Brock's 182 right now. Lila's here with me. All right." He spoke to Lila. "She's gotten permission to go to the tower. She'll be coming by to pick you up on her way." He handed her the phone. "She's going to need you. We'll be in touch by radio."

Brock hollered at one of his crew, "Barney, c'mon, let's roll out that Skylane, we've got an emergency!"

As Dr. Cooper ran out to help roll out the airplane, he called to Lila over his shoulder, "Pray for us."

Lila nodded to her father as she spoke into the telephone. "Hello? Aunt Joyce?"

Chuck had been crisscrossing and circling a mile from the cloud that had swallowed up the Skylane, trying to see any sign of it and listening to the radio communications between Jay and Barbara Maxwell.

"Okay," came Jay's voice. "I've given it a little more power."

"Give it a touch of right aileron," said Barbara. "We want to make this turn nice and easy."

In the tower, Maxwell and Parker gazed steadfastly at the radar screen.

"Come on, pal, you can do it," said Parker.

Maxwell nodded happily. "Yes, the turn looks good and the altitude is holding . . . now he's climbing a little . . . two thousand eight hundred feet and still climbing."

Parker spoke to Chuck, "Eight Eight Niner, be looking, the Skylane should be coming out of those clouds at ten o'clock at two thousand eight hundred."

Chuck pressed up against the window of the Cub, his eyes sweeping the sky for any sign of The Yank. He could see the cloud, and below its fringes the first gradual slopes of the Cascade foothills, but so far. . . .

There it was, appearing like a tiny white angel out of heaven!

"YES!" Chuck yelled, then radioed, "I have the Skylane!"

"Okay," said the tower, "he's all yours again."

Ben Parker allowed himself a quick little smile as he gave Barbara Maxwell a thumbs-up. She eased back in her chair and rubbed her face with her hands.

"Okay, Eight Eight Niner," said Parker, "use one radio to talk to Mr. Jay Cooper and one radio to listen to us. We have information on the autopilot."

He signaled Josie Fleming, who spoke through her headset as she referred to some scribbled notes at her desk. "Eight Eight Niner, the Skylane has an autopilot, single axis only. It's located at the bottom center of the panel, just above the power quadrant. . . ."

Chuck listened and passed the information on to Jay. "Jay, your airplane has an autopilot. It won't do all the flying, but it'll keep the wings level for you, and that's half the battle right now. You know where the throttle is, right? Those four knobs in a row?"

Jay felt for the four knobs. By now they were easy to find by touch. "Okay, now what?"

"Just above those knobs there's a squarish box with a knob in the middle and two little flat switches on either side of that."

Jay groped for it with his left hand. "Yeah . . . I think I found it."

"Touch right, Jay, you're turning again."

Jay carefully repeated that little procedure for the umpteenth time.

Chuck continued, "That knob should pull out about a quarter of an inch. See if it does."

Jay found the knob and gave it a tug. It came out with a click. "Yeah, I've pulled it out."

"Great. That was the wing leveler. Now, that little flat switch on the left side should turn it on. Flip it up."

Jay found the switch and flipped it upward with a click.

He was startled when the yoke in his hands twisted with a jerk. He held it tight and it seemed to squirm under his grip.

"Jay?"

"Something's . . . the yoke is wiggling."

Chuck flopped back in his seat and grinned toward heaven. "It's the autopilot, Jay! You did it!"

"Am I turning?" Jay asked, with a tense voice.

Chuck watched as the Skylane flew past him and he turned to follow. "No, you're just fine, flying straight and level. Good job!"

In the control tower, Parker and his crew heard it all and breathed one little sigh of relief—temporary relief. They still had to get that plane safely on the ground.

Josie Fleming was on the telephone, talking to Joyce. "That's right, just ring the buzzer at the big glass door. Someone will be down to let you in." She reported to Ben Parker, "The pilot's wife and niece are on their way here."

"Good," said Parker. "They need to be here, whatever happens."

Within minutes, Skylane 359ZM—pronounced Three Five Niner Zulu Mike—took to the air with Brock Axley in the left seat as pilot and Dr. Cooper in the right seat.

"Boeing Tower," Brock radioed, "Skylane Niner Zulu Mike with you, climbing through fifteen hundred."

Ben Parker replied, "Roger, Niner Zulu Mike, radar contact. Eight Yankee Tango is now westbound at three thousand and climbing slowly. You are cleared into Class Bravo airspace. Fly heading one three five to intercept. Advise when you have traffic." The "Class Bravo" airspace was normally restricted to commercial airline traffic flying in and out of Seattle-Tacoma International. For now, the two Skylanes and the little Piper Cub had that airspace all to themselves.

"Niner Zulu Mike," came the reply from Brock Axley.

Next Parker added, "Also, be advised that Eight Yankee Tango is now on single axis autopilot."

Brock exchanged a glance with Dr. Cooper as he radioed back, "Thanks. That's good news."

"Roger that."

Dr. Cooper searched the sky through binoculars. "Don't see him yet."

Brock was somber. "This is going to be a tough one, Jake. I don't know of anyone who's ever flown a plane blind, much less landed it."

Dr. Cooper lowered the binoculars and continued to look ahead as he grappled with that very question. "Well . . . there's always a first time."

"Jake—"

Dr. Cooper looked at his friend. "There's hope, Brock. Jay's flown our plane several times. He knows how to maneuver and how to land."

"Yeah, but blind? Jake, even an instrument pilot has to have eyes to read his instruments. There's no way Jay can tell what that airplane is doing."

Dr. Cooper thought for only a moment and then replied, "Well, he's still alive and The Yank is still flying. With God's help, we'll just have to be Jay's eyes, that's all."

"Okay, it's stable, on autopilot, so we've got a little time to work on the problem," said Ben Parker. "Josie, what's the fuel situation?"

Fleming was working out numbers on her calculator and tapping keys on her computer. "The flight plan says Eight Yankee Tango left with three hours of fuel in the tanks. Kramer opened the flight plan at twelve thirty p.m., and it's now—" she looked at the clock on the wall "two in the afternoon."

Parker nodded. He called Brock and Dr. Cooper through his headset. "Niner Zulu Mike, we figure Eight Yankee Tango has about one and a half hours of fuel left. Do you have the plane in sight?"

Aboard Niner Zulu Mike, Dr. Cooper gazed through his binoculars and replied, "Yeah, we've got him, westbound at our altitude. We should be able to come alongside in just a few minutes."

"Okay, contact him on the Auburn frequency but monitor our frequency so we can get through to you. And by the way, make sure the boy can't hear us talking to each other. We'll be discussing some pretty heavy topics."

"Roger. Understand," said Brock.

By now they could see The Yank without binoculars, a small white object moving from left to right across their windshield. Brock started a gradual right turn and increased power to catch up and come alongside.

Dr. Cooper switched to the Auburn frequency. "Jay, it's Dad. Can you hear me?"

Jay's blind eyes got wide. "Dad? Where are you?"

Dr. Cooper couldn't help smiling at the sound of his son's voice. "We're chasing you in another 182. We can see you up ahead and we're catching up with you right now."

Brock pointed to the east. "There's Chuck Westmore."

Dr. Cooper could see the faithful little Piper Cub coming their way but falling far behind the Skylane once again. "Eight Eight Niner, hello. This is Skylane Three Five Niner Zulu Mike."

"Hello, and a thousand welcomes!" Chuck replied. "They told me you were coming. I can see you at one o'clock."

"And we have you in sight. This is Jake Cooper,

Jay's Dad. I've heard about you from my brother-in-law. I'd sure like to meet you and shake your hand when this is all over."

Chuck was more than just relieved to see the other airplane arrive. He was overjoyed. "And I'll want to shake yours. That's a wonderful, brave young man you have there."

"Well, with your help he's still alive and we're going to try to get him down."

"He's all yours. I'm running low on fuel and I have to get out of here."

"We've got him. Thanks, and be praying for us."

"Absolutely. Good day."

As Chuck turned for home he caught one last glimpse of The Yank far ahead, its wings shining in the afternoon sun, with the other Skylane turning after it, almost becoming its shadow.

"Dear God," he prayed, "bring a happy ending to this day."

Brock brought Niner Zulu Mike to a position about two hundred feet to the left of The Yank and brought back his speed to keep the two airplanes flying in a rough formation.

Dr. Cooper peered through the binoculars and could see Rex's body slumped against the left window, his chin down on his chest. "Jay," he radioed, "has Rex moved at all?"

"I don't think so," Jay's voice sounded weak and his words were mumbled.

"How about breathing and pulse?"

Jay's head was swimming. A terrible nausea and numbness were continuing to creep into his body and he couldn't shake them off. "I . . . I'll try to check." Weakly, shakily, he reached over and explored for his uncle's wrist. He pressed his fingers against the veins to feel for a pulse, but no sensation would come through. "I can't feel anything . . . my fingers are all tingly. . . ."

"Jay, how are *you?*" Dr. Cooper asked.

"I'm sick," Jay answered in a mumbling voice. "I'm real sick. I feel like I'm going to throw up, and I'm all dizzy, and my hands are numb."

Brock shook his head. "Airsickness. He's got it bad." He radioed, "Jay, this is Brock Axley, your uncle's airplane mechanic. Try to sit back and hold still. Hold your head up straight and don't move around a lot. Breathe evenly, not too much, not too little. Jay, you doing that?"

"Okay," Jay weakly replied.

"Can you get the window open? It'll help you feel better and the cool air might wake up Rex."

"I'll try," Jay said.

Jay knew how to open the window . . . at least, at one time he did. Right now his mind wasn't clicking too well. He reached up with a right hand that felt very heavy and found the window latch. He worked it loose, and the window popped open. At once a blast of cool air rushed through the cabin. It felt good.

A telephone in the control tower rang and Johnny Adair picked it up. "Oh, hello. Yes, okay, we're expecting you." He called to Ben Parker, "Mrs. Kramer and the boy's sister are downstairs."

Parker replied, "Johnny, go down there and personally show them to the employees' lounge. Anything they want—food, coffee, a minister, whatever—make sure they get it. Tune in the radio scanner so they can hear what's going on. Stick around to answer their questions." He hesitated just a little out of regret, but then added, "If they want to come up here give them our apologies. But don't allow them up here."

Adair headed for the stairs. "Will do."

"Johnny!" Parker called after him, and Adair halted. "That scanner down there. Set it to the Auburn frequency, 122.8. They can hear the two planes talking to each other, but I don't want them hearing Axley and Cooper talking with us."

Adair nodded grimly. "Gotcha."

After Adair left, Parker explained to the others, "We all know it's entirely possible that the boy and his uncle are going to die today. The family doesn't need to hear the downside."

46

FOUR

Johnny Adair took the elevator down to the street level and opened the big glass door to let Joyce and Lila come through. He took them up to the employees' lounge on the fourth floor, a comfortable room with couches, chairs, a few tables, a sink, a coffee machine, and a tray of leftover donuts from that morning.

"Um, we'll order out for anything else you want to eat. I'm here to take care of all that."

He showed them a small radio sitting on a round table in the center of the room. "This is a radio scanner. I'll set it to the Auburn frequency, and you'll be able to hear the two airplanes talking to each other."

"Thank you," said Joyce, taking a chair next to the table. Immediately she reached into her purse and took out her own portable scanner. "And what frequency is the tower using?"

Adair hesitated and looked nervous. "Uh . . . I don't, uh . . ."

"I was listening to the emergency frequency on my way over." Joyce clicked on the scanner, and they immediately heard Dr. Cooper's voice: "Boeing

47

Tower, we're on the right side of Eight Yankee Tango, and I can see the passenger."

As Adair stood there speechless, Lila pulled up another chair and joined her aunt in listening to the two scanners. During the next hours they would strain to hear every word.

Brock had flown his plane up, over, and then down on the other side of The Yank so they could get a better look at Jay through the passenger window.

Dr. Cooper looked through his binoculars. The sight turned his stomach. He could see his son slouched in the passenger seat, his head resting against the seat back, his mouth hanging open as if he were gasping for air, and his forehead, cheek, and neck smeared with a stream of blood.

"Dear Lord . . . ," he said softly.

He lowered the binoculars, sat back in his seat, and stared straight ahead, stunned, trying to recover from a sudden wave of fear and despair.

Brock could see the boy's blood-stained face even without the binoculars. He kept the airplane steady while he touched Dr. Cooper's arm. "Easy, Jake. It isn't over yet."

Dr. Cooper gathered himself and nodded. He pressed the talk button on his control yoke and said again, "We can see the passenger."

Joyce and Lila leaned close to hear Dr. Cooper report, "Jay has some kind of head injury. His face is streaked with blood." Lila made a conscious effort to be strong even as she unconsciously covered her mouth with her hands. She could see her Aunt Joyce's hands trembling, clasped before her on the table. They could hear the stress in Dr. Cooper's voice as he continued, "He appears very weak and he's complaining of nausea and numbness in his hands. We told him to open the window for some air and he was able to do that."

Joyce grabbed Lila's hand as one word formed on her lips in a whisper: "Jesus."

Ben Parker paced, his hands on his hips, his brow furrowed with a difficult decision. Finally he radioed, "Zulu Mike, do what you can to guide the aircraft out over Puget Sound . . ." He loathed the words even as he said them, "and keep it there." He released his talk button so they wouldn't hear him speak his reason: "We don't want it crashing into any people or houses."

Brock eased Zulu Mike away from Rex's airplane a safe distance and told Dr. Cooper, "It's all yours, Jake."

Dr. Cooper switched to the other radio and pressed the talk button. "Jay, you still with us?"

Jay felt he was dreaming, about to pass out any moment. A hammer pounded on his head with each pulse of his heartbeat, and for all he knew, his hands had fallen off and were lying on the floor somewhere. Weird visions were playing through his head, swirling and pulsing in the darkened theater of his blindness.

"Jay?" his father's voice sternly called again. "Jay, come in."

Somehow he found the talk button on the yoke in front of him. He pressed it, and muttered, "Hello."

"Jay, we're heading out over Puget Sound right now. We're still climbing just a bit, almost to four thousand feet so we'll have lots of nice, safe sky under us. You hear me?"

Something about hearing his father's voice brought Jay a new strength. "Yeah, Dad. Just keep talking."

"Now son, we're all hoping and praying that Rex will come around, but if he doesn't, you'll have to fly the airplane."

Jay figured his father must not know. "Dad, I can't see!"

"I know, son. But we're working out a plan to get you down. I'm going to pray for us, okay? You don't have to say anything, just listen."

Jay closed his eyes to pray. The dull, fuzzy light before his eyes went black—except for that, closing his eyes looked no different than having them open.

His father started to pray. "Dear Lord, we are in Your hands today. We pray for Your strength and Your courage. . . ."

In the employees' lounge, Lila and Joyce clasped hands and prayed along, drawing strength from their faith and from each other.

In the control tower, Ben Parker and his crew heard Dr. Cooper's prayer coming over the loud-speaker: ". . . we pray for Rex, that You will help him recover and wake up to pilot the airplane. But if not, we pray that You will strengthen Jay and open his eyes so he can do what needs to be done."

Barbara Maxwell kept her eyes glued on the radar screen, but she was praying along. Josie Fleming stared at the weather briefing on her computer screen, but she too was praying. Bob Konishi was not a religious man, but he certainly agreed with the words he heard.

Dr. Cooper concluded, ". . . We ask all this in Your precious name, Amen."

In the control tower, Ben Parker was staring grimly out the window. His crew of air-traffic controllers could not tell if he was praying. But at Dr. Cooper's amen, Parker echoed firmly, "Amen," then addressed them all.

"This is a government facility and you are all

federal employees. For the record, no one is required to pray, but if anyone so desires, they won't get any static from me. Just pray with your eyes open so you can do your job." He looked skyward to indicate his thoughts were with the young lad, bleeding and blind. "The federal government can't help that boy now. Only God can."

Even though still in great pain, Jay felt a peace come over him, and he thanked God for it. It was a familiar feeling he'd known before. He and his family had been through plenty of tough adventures, but they never went through them alone. He knew they wouldn't be alone this time either.

His father's voice came through his headset, "God bless and keep you, son."

Jay smiled a weak smile. "Thanks, Dad. Don't worry. We'll make it."

"So let's check you out on the controls. Ready?"

A touch of faith helped ease Jay's fear; the sound of his father's voice brought him comfort; and having something constructive to do brought him hope. "Let's do it."

"Let's see where the throttle controls are set. Can you find them?"

Jay's mind cleared just enough to reach with his left hand and find the four knobs in a row. "Uh . . . carb heat, throttle, prop, and mixture."

His father was chuckling with delight as he

responded, "All right, real good. Now let's get all the knobs except the throttle pushed all the way in."

Jay felt carefully for each knob, the pain throbbing in his head as he made the effort. "Carb heat . . . all the way in. Throttle. . . ."

"Just leave that alone for now."

"Okay. Uhhh . . . prop all the way in."

"Good."

"Mixture all the way in."

"All right. Now stand by."

Jay eased back in his seat again just to rest, hoping and praying his head would stop hurting and his stomach would finally settle down.

Brock rechecked the throttle arrangement in his own airplane. "Okay. We're maintaining one hundred thirty knots and able to stay alongside him. His throttle must be close to a cruise setting."

"Which gives him less than an hour and a half of fuel," Cooper mused.

"Throttling back will buy him another half hour or so."

Dr. Cooper radioed Jay, "Jay, we're going to slow you down. Can you find the trim wheel?"

Joyce studied Lila's face. The young girl seemed frozen with fear, her eyes staring intensely at nothing. "Lila? Lila, what are they doing?"

Lila snapped out of her stupor and looked at Joyce. "They're . . . I think they're trying to save some fuel."

Joyce already knew that, but she felt she should keep Lila talking, explaining. At least it would make her a part of all that was happening. "How? I need you to explain it to me."

Lila had to think. It calmed her. "I think they're trying to save fuel. An airplane burns more fuel going fast than going slow, just like a car. So I bet they're going to have him pull the throttle back to make the fuel last longer."

"And what's the trim wheel? What's that for?"

Lila began to tense up again. Her eyes became glassy and her hands were shaking.

Joyce pressed her question. "Come on, I need to know."

Lila worked to produce an answer. "If Jay pulls the throttle back without trimming, the airplane won't slow down, it'll just descend. If he pulls the throttle back and then uses the trim wheel to pitch the nose up, the plane will slow down but stay up."

Joyce gave Lila a teasing little poke. "I thought you didn't care for flying."

Lila shrugged. "I figured if I was going to be riding with my Dad and Jay in our airplane, I'd better know what to do if something terrible happened . . ." Her voice trailed off and pain filled her face. "Like right now."

Joyce touched her shoulder. "Hey, Lila, come on, now . . ."

Lila swallowed a wave of emotion and said, "I should have gone with them. I could have been there. I could have helped."

Joyce gripped her shoulder. "You're helping me. We're helping each other. That counts for a lot."

Lila reached up and gripped Joyce's hand on her shoulder. Together they continued to listen.

There were other people in the Seattle area with radio scanners: the television and radio stations, the newspapers, anyone whose job it was to know when something newsworthy was happening. As soon as a radio call went out for emergency vehicles at Boeing Field, the media people heard it. The telephones at the tower began to ring incessantly. Media vehicles began to arrive, cluttering up the parking area in front of the control tower. First came the small white vans and station wagons with big logos painted on their sides— News 7, Channel 4, Eyewitness 11—bringing in a multitude of reporters and camerapeople. Right behind them came the big news trucks with satellite dishes atop their roofs. All of this was attracting the attention from passing motorists, who stopped to follow the story. And they were all taking up a lot of space.

"The media are storming the place," Johnny

Adair reported as he came up the stairs into the control room.

"Get the airport manager on that one," said Ben Parker. "We're busy."

"I just talked to him," said Adair. "He wants somebody from the tower to tell the press what's going on."

Parker rolled his eyes. "Okay, Johnny, that's you."

Adair wasn't ready for that. "But . . . what do I —

"You're the go-between. Answer their questions, give them interviews, appear on camera, do whatever you have to. Just keep them out of our hair."

Adair replied "Will do," and headed down the stairs.

Parker looked out at the sky. "Any moment the choppers are going to be calling."

Bob Konishi waved. "I've got Channel Seven's news chopper on the radio."

"Yep, here they come."

"And now I'm getting a call from Channel Eleven. Same thing. They want permission to televise the two airplanes."

Parker smiled resignedly and shook his head. "Give them a squawk code so we can tell which radar blip they are. They have permission to approach within one mile, they are to see and avoid all traffic, and make sure they know that if they get any closer than that I'm going to bust them from here to tomorrow."

Konishi smiled. "I'll tell them."

All over the Pacific Northwest the network soap operas and game shows were bumped off the air by the drama taking place in the skies over Puget Sound. Television images from cameras aboard the news helicopters showed the two Skylanes flying in formation as reporters and news anchors narrated over the picture: ". . . a beautiful setting for such a tense drama . . . with limited fuel and slim chances for a successful landing, the young man's father in the white and green Skylane is now trying to teach his son in the white and red Skylane how to fly the airplane. . . ."

A reporter on the television asked Adair, "What are the chances that this young man with limited flying experience will be able to safely land the airplane?"

Adair hesitated and fumbled, staring at his notes as if he might find the answer there. Finally he answered, "I'd rather not comment on that. If you'll excuse me now, I have to get back to the tower. We'll keep you posted."

In the tower employees' lounge, Lila and Joyce were watching the news coverage, including live pictures of the two airplanes, on the lounge television. Adair had allowed a limited number of reporters into the room, and they were quite eager to hear Lila's comment. She turned from the television and looked directly at them as she answered, "I've seen my brother do a lot of wild things. With God's help, he'll make it."

As Jay sat in that noisy airplane without eyesight, every little motion of the airplane sent him a different message: *you're turning, you're sinking, you're climbing, you're slowing down, speeding up, flipping over . . .*

Jay could only be sure of one thing: all this motion, real or not, was making him sick, and not just *kind of* sick. He was way past *kind of* sick and tumbling headlong into *seriously* sick with no hope of putting it off any longer, much less recovering. The fresh air blowing in the open window no longer helped. Sitting still and relaxing no longer helped. The sound of his father's voice could no longer calm his stomach or bring clarity to his mind.

I'm going to lose it, he thought. *I'm going to conk out.* In a last desperate move, he returned the autopilot knob to center, wings level.

Then a deeper kind of darkness settled over him and he slumped over, his head drooping, his chest suspended against the shoulder restraint. The noise of the airplane ebbed from his consciousness along with all the pain.

Dr. Cooper saw Jay slump over. "Jay! Jay, come in!"

There was no response.

Dr. Cooper grabbed his binoculars and got a

closer look at his son. "Oh no. He's out, Brock. He's passed out."

Brock took back the binoculars from Dr. Cooper and focused on Jay. He pressed his talk button and called, "Jay! Jay, come on now. Snap out of it. Heads up."

The boy didn't stir or respond.

Brock looked at Dr. Cooper, who could only return his horrified expression. They both knew what this could mean.

Skylane Eight Yankee Tango continued westward at four thousand feet, straight and level on auto-pilot, and with both occupants unconscious. Up ahead were the Olympic Mountains; beyond them, the Pacific Ocean.

And now there was no way to turn The Yank around.

FIVE

Ben Parker listened to Dr. Cooper's report with a stony grimness. "Roger, Niner Zulu Mike, we copy that."

There was a deathlike silence in the control tower. The other controllers had heard Dr. Cooper's report and were stunned. Finally, Bob Konishi voiced the question they were all wondering, "So what now?"

Parker asked Barbara Maxwell, "Which way is it heading?"

Maxwell glanced at her radar screen. "Course is two six five."

Josie Fleming was already unfolding an aviation chart and spreading it out on her desk. "Course two six five," she repeated, laying a plotter on the chart and drawing a line to indicate the airplane's path. "Ninety knots . . . one and a half hours of fuel. . . ."

Parker came up to her table to have a look. "What about those mountains?"

Josie Fleming ran a nervous finger over her hair and whistled a quiet sigh. "At four thousand feet it'll be close. The plane's flight path passes close to some mountains of more than five thousand feet. If he misses those peaks, he'll continue out until he's over the ocean." She took out a calculator and tapped in some numbers. "About sixty miles beyond the coastline, to be more exact. He'll be in international waters."

Parker shook his head. Fleming continued, "It all depends on how straight Yankee Tango flies. I don't think they had the boy set the autopilot to hold a heading, but just to keep the wings level. All it takes is a gust of wind or some turbulence to nudge that plane to a different course."

"And hit the mountains," Parker stated.

"Either that or crash in the ocean." Sorrowfully, Fleming shook her head. "If somebody in that airplane doesn't wake up, I guess it won't matter which one happens."

Brock and Dr. Cooper kept following alongside Eight Yankee Tango, praying, watching for any stirring inside the cabin, and wishing there was something else they could do.

"Wish I could walk over there, open that stupid door, and climb in and fly that thing!" Brock said in frustration and anger.

Dr. Cooper could see the Olympic Mountains looming ahead. He switched to the tower radio. "Boeing Tower, any ideas? We are rapidly approaching the mountains."

Ben Parker was pacing around the control room, thinking, scowling. "Stand by, Zulu Mike, we're working on it."

Bob Konishi let out a loud sigh, tapping his desk-top impatiently. "Working on what?"

Parker was angry. "Options, Bob, options! Let's go through our options and if we have to come up with more, we will. There must be a way to keep the plane from hitting the mountains."

"Or landing in the ocean," Fleming added.

Parker shot a glance at Fleming. "Suppose it does land in the ocean. What are the chances of survival?"

"None," she responded. "Right now the plane's trimmed for ninety knots. That's the speed at which it'll hit the water, steeply nose down. Upon impact it will either nose over, cartwheel, or both. In any case it'll disintegrate and the passengers won't survive." Her face sank into a genuinely remorseful expression. "And even if we could somehow make a controlled landing, these planes don't float. There's a real question whether the occupants would be strong enough to escape the cockpit before the airplane sinks. We know the pilot won't be able to get out unless he wakes up. As for the kid, who knows *what* condition he's in?"

Konishi concluded, "The Coast Guard is ready with a chopper, but all they can do at this point is follow the plane, wait for it to crash—wherever it crashes—and then do what they can."

Parker's eyes narrowed as he scanned the room. "Okay, let's reach a bit. Think of something outlandish. It could still work, you never know."

"Okay," said Konishi, "how about lowering a pilot from another airplane?"

"It's a high-wing light aircraft," Fleming objected. "The doors are under the wing. The guy being lowered couldn't get to them. Besides that, if you open a door on a plane that size, the door becomes a rudder and throws the plane sideways. Then there's the problem of the two front seats being full of bodies. How's the guy going to pack himself in there?" Exasperated, she added, "And finally, he'd be only a few feet from a spinning prop that could cut him to pieces if a gust of wind wiggled him or the airplane the wrong direction. . . . Oh, and after that, the prop will be ruined and the plane will crash."

"So, forget the pilot. Just lower a hook or something and grab the airplane out of the sky."

Fleming thought Konishi was kidding. "Oh yeah, *right!*"

"No, now wait a minute." Parker said, raising his hand. They all stopped to listen. "That could be it. A chopper with a skyhook, a sling, something to grab the airplane, maybe lasso it around the tail section."

Fleming was about to object, but stopped short.

"How about it, Fleming?"

She gave half a shrug. "Might work. Tons of risk, though. A light plane is pretty small up there in the sky. You couldn't just lasso it. Somebody would have to be lowered on a harness to attach the sling, encountering the risks we've already mentioned. Meanwhile, the rotor wash from the chopper could throw the plane out of control. And then, as far as attaching anything to the tail section, it would have to be done without touching the tail fin or stabilizer. Any force or weight from a full-grown body back there would be enough to throw the airplane completely out of control. And if you want the sling around the tail section, that will probably damage the airplane so it would not be able to fly."

"So we'll only get one shot at it," Parker said grimly.

She leaned back and thoughtfully tapped her desk with her pencil. "Once that sling goes around the tail section, there's no turning back. Keep in mind the plane's engine is still running. If the chopper can snag the Skylane, it'll have a live fish on the line, buzzing around in circles and pulling. But if the chopper can handle that—"

Parker slapped his desktop. "I say it's worth a try. Bob, get the Coast Guard on the phone. Tell them we need their biggest chopper and somebody's who's crazy enough to try it."

Dr. Cooper consulted his aeronautical chart. "That peak up ahead is five thousand fifty-four feet. The one beyond it is four thousand nine hundred sixty feet."

"We're at four thousand two hundred fifty, right now," said Brock.

"Jay, wake up," Cooper radioed. But Jay remained slumped against the window.

"Well, you never know," said Brock. "Yankee Tango might pass to one side of those peaks."

"Oh Lord, make it happen," Dr. Cooper prayed.

It was a different sensation having the ground come up to meet them instead of descending to the ground themselves. Below them, the mountain slopes began to rise and the treetops began to pass under them closer and faster. Straight ahead, the view of a forested ridge filled the windshield.

Brock finally pushed in the throttle. "We've got to climb or we won't make it over that thing."

Dr. Cooper craned his neck to keep The Yank in sight. He could see it below them now, purring along at a steady altitude, heading for the ridge.

Aboard Eight Yankee Tango, Rex Kramer sat motionless, chin on his chest, the victim of a severe concussion, while Jay Cooper remained slumped over in a faint. The altimeter indicated four thousand three hundred feet. The very tops of tall firs and hemlocks began to appear now and again outside the windows as the mountain rose up beneath them. The airplane began to wobble in air rippling like stream water over the ridge. The ground below reached to four thousand feet, then climbed to four thousand two hundred. Now the tallest treetops nearly brushed The Yank's wheels.

The fact that Eight Yankee Tango was coming nose to nose with a mountain ridge was not wasted on the news reporters in the choppers. The reporter riding in Channel 11's helicopter spoke rapidly in a strained, high-pitched voice, "This does not look good . . . it does not look good. The aircraft is flying too low to clear that ridge. We might have a crash any moment. It does not look good!"

Joyce and Lila kept watching, praying, their eyes glued to the TV screen.

Aboard Niner Zulu Mike, both Dr. Cooper and Brock Axley held their breath as they watched Eight Yankee Tango skimming over the ridge, approaching the crest.

"Come on, come on," said Dr. Cooper, "you can make it."

There were tall trees ahead and just to the right of The Yank's path. To the left, the ground dropped away and there was a treeless field of crumbled rock.

"That rock field," said Brock. "Fly over the rock field!"

Eight Yankee Tango skimmed over the top of one grove of trees, its prop wash making the branches quiver. A rocky outcropping passed close under the right wing, a stubby tree under the left.

Straight ahead, a stand of tall hemlocks formed a deadly wall along the crest of the ridge. The Yank kept flying headlong toward them. Jay remained unconscious, with no idea that trees and sharp stones were passing by at ninety knots only a few feet below him.

The reporter in the chopper spoke into his microphone while speaking to the plane, "Come on, come on, don't crash now!"

Aboard Niner Zulu Mike, Dr. Cooper grasped the edge of the instrument panel with such a fierce grip that his fingernails made permanent marks.

Yankee Tango shuddered as a flow of air moved up over the sun-warmed rocks and boiled under its right wing. The wing raised for a moment. The nose moved to the left. The autopilot leveled the wings again. The top of a low pine gently slapped the left wheel. The plane fishtailed to the left.

The wall of hemlocks came up on the right as the airplane's shadow raced over the rocks. The hemlocks were only inches from touching the wheels. The propeller was kicking up dust. Chipmunks ran for cover. The right wing clipped the tip of a branch, slipped between two more, and passed over a low scrub.

"Don't crash, please don't crash!" Dr. Cooper hissed through clenched teeth.

The reporter in Channel 11's helicopter held his microphone in a white-knuckled grip, so tense he had no words.

The Yank's right tire touched the tip of a rock, raising a tiny puff of dust. The right wingtip passed by one last tree, so close that the tree shuddered.

And then the airplane cleared the ridge. The ground, the rocks, the trees all dropped away far below. Eight Yankee Tango was flying in open sky once more.

And Dr. Cooper fell back into his seat, limp with relief, shaking.

"Yes!" the reporter on chopper seven shouted.

"He made it!" said Channel 4's reporter.

"More time now for Skylane Eight Yankee Tango as the world watches," mused the man on Channel 11.

Joyce and Lila suddenly found themselves embraced and touched by a tangled web of arms and hands. The people in the lounge were all breathing again.

"That was the quickest touch-and-go I ever saw," Brock quipped.

Dr. Cooper laughed, and it felt good.

Then, suddenly, Brock exclaimed, "What in the world?"

"On no," yelled Dr. Cooper. "Now what?"

Brock pointed to the south. Dr. Cooper's eyes grew wide.

Closing in from the south was something more than just a helicopter. This had to be the biggest, ugliest machine available, with two black rotors whirling and wop-wop-wopping overhead and a massive, big-bellied fuselage painted orange and white. It looked like some oversized mutant insect from a monster movie, big enough to pick up a house.

"The Coast Guard!" Dr. Cooper exclaimed.

Right on cue, the Boeing tower called. "Niner Zulu Mike, you have additional traffic at eight o'clock, same altitude, a Coast Guard helicopter. Help's on the way."

Brock responded, "Roger, we have traffic," then just kept staring. "What in the world are they going to do?"

Dr. Cooper pressed his talk button and asked, "Uh, Boeing Tower, just what are the chopper's intentions?"

Ben Parker was waiting as Johnny Adair set up still another television in the control room so the controllers could see what was going on. "Niner Zulu Mike, the Coast Guard is going to try to snag Yankee Tango with a cable and winch. Give them plenty of room and hope that all goes well."

Aboard chopper Two Zero Bravo, pilot Abe Weinstein radioed back, "Roger, Two Zero Bravo in position and ready to proceed." Then he switched to the chopper intercom. "Okay, Carson, whenever you're ready."

In the deep belly of the chopper, Lieutenant David Carson, Coast Guard career man, zipped up his heavy flight suit, fastened his helmet strap, and double-checked the harness and cable by which he would be lowered to the Skylane. The big side door was open. A ninety-knot blast of air was roaring around through the chopper's insides. Two hundred feet below them and trailing behind was the 182, close, but frighteningly small, like a model airplane, rocking just a little from the downblast of the chopper's blades but otherwise holding a steady course. Below the Skylane, the distant treetops of the Olympic rainforest moved slowly backward.

"How's it looking, Billings?" he asked through a helmet radio.

Seaman Tommy Billings was the winch man. He was standing at his post by the open door, his heavy flight suit and helmet protecting him from the wind. He was preparing a second cable with a large loop in the end resembling a cowboy's lasso. "Just like the rodeo, only this steer's flying."

Carson was putting on a parachute, just in case. "So we'll see if I make a very good cowboy."

"That Skylane's bucking a bit. You won't be able to get real close." Carson stood at Billings's side and looked down at the small white-winged airplane. He could see it swaying a little, dipping, wagging. Billings clipped the cable lasso to Carson's belt.

"I'll lower you down as close as I can. When you're ready, loop this around the tail section and then we'll pull you out of the way. The instant the cable tightens around that bird it's going to fight us like a trout on a hook. You don't want to be anywhere near it," Billings said.

Carson stepped to the threshold. "Okay, let's go." He stepped out into the wind, swinging free on the end of the cable. With a little wave of good-bye and good luck, Billings started lowering him to the plane.

"There he is!" someone in the lounge shouted, and everyone leaned toward the television screens as Carson's small body appeared out of the belly of the huge chopper then began dangling at the end of a cable. His body was quickly swept back behind the chopper by the wind.

Brock and Dr. Cooper watched without a word. Dr. Cooper could feel the uneasiness, the pure terror of this moment. Yet, at the same time he felt a sense of awe to see such courage.

Carson felt like a kite in the wind, his flight suit fluttering in the blast, the wind a dull roar outside his helmet. He found he could direct his body slightly to the left or right by extending his arms and legs like a sky diver, and the longer the cable got, the bigger a swing he could accomplish. He could not see the Skylane. He was facing forward, and it was down there somewhere behind him.

"How far to go?" he radioed Billings.

"You'll see it right below you any second," Billings replied. "We're trying to keep you above that prop."

"I appreciate that." Just then, the nose of the airplane appeared below his feet. "Okay! I've got the nose right under me, about twenty feet down. Keep bringing me back."

As the cable played out and Carson watched, the airplane seemed to advance under him, the prop a blurring, spinning disk on edge. He could hear the hiss of the knife-edged propeller blades. Next he could see the windshield, and the legs of the two injured occupants inside. "Yeah, I can see some blood on the boy's legs, and there's some blood on the windshield in front of the pilot." Now he was above the white wings, so close he could read the little placards next to the fuel caps: 100 LL Only. The wings were rocking and wagging a little, upset by the chopper's rotors.

"Okay," he radioed, "almost to the tail section."

He continued to move steadily backward and downward until the tail section was directly below him. "Okay, I'm there. It's about ten feet below me. And it's moving, all right. It'll be like trying to rope a wild horse."

Carson was used to dropping down to rescue people off sinking boats, but usually the boats weren't moving, there was no ninety-knot wind, and the cable was straight up and down. In this case *everything* was moving, and in the rotor wash of the chopper and the blast of the oncoming wind, both the Skylane and Carson were being tossed around like two wild kites. First the tail section was directly below him, then it moved off to his left, and then to his right. All the while it was bucking up and down in a frightening, unpredictable manner. It was like stalking a two thousand pound butterfly, wondering if it would ever hold still so he could catch it. He grabbed the cable lasso and unclipped it from his belt, holding it in his right hand.

"Can you lower the chopper?"

"Working on it," came pilot Weinstein's voice.

Carson had no sense of descending. Instead, the Skylane seemed to rise toward him, still shifting, rocking, wagging its tail. He spread the loop of cable open with his left hand, his eyes on that tail section, looking for that one precise moment of opportunity. If he could loop the cable gently around the right stabilizer first, then over the tail, then the left stabilizer . . . if he could somehow get his body farther to the right . . . if he and the plane would hold still. . . .

He was close now, so close the tail fin was waving just below his face, swinging like a gate in the wind, back and forth, up and down. If he wasn't careful it would knock his face shield off. "Good, good, that's low enough." He held the lasso ready, watching for his chance. . . .

An updraft! The tail came up at him like an angry shark fin! Instinctively he curled his body to the right and the tip of the fin struck his left shoulder, flipping him over on his back. Now he was facing backwards, the airplane behind his head. The rudder scraped across the top of his helmet as he kicked and struggled, trying to turn rightside up, trying to see where he was. A sudden and forceful jerk on the cable flipped him over again. Now he was facing forward, and to his horror he discovered the cable to his harness was snarled in a radio antenna on the top of the tail fin. "STEADY, STEADY! I'm snarled in the antenna!"

His weight brought the cable down hard on the tail fin, the tail section lowered, the airplane nosed up and started climbing, he and the cable held the tail section down so it nosed up even steeper. He could see the arc of the prop cutting ever closer to the cable.

Got to get the weight off this cable! His left hand went to his chest, found the quick release, *pulled*.

The cable came loose and he fell backward in a free fall. The cable, free of his weight, snaked and whipped above the Skylane.

Billings saw it all and hollered to the pilot, "Take her up, take her up! Abort! Veer to the left, the left!"

Weinstein pulled hard on the control stick, and the huge chopper clawed for more sky as the Skylane, its nose raised awkwardly, gained altitude but lost speed, fading back.

With great relief, Billings saw both Carson's cable and the lasso cable whip free of the plane and trail in the wind harmlessly above it. Far back and far below, a brightly striped parachute popped open.

"Carson! You all right?"

Carson radioed back, "I'm okay. How's the airplane?"

Even as Carson asked the question, Billings saw the airplane, its airspeed exhausted by the abrupt climb, nose over into a dive.

"It's going down, Carson! It's out of control! I think we crippled it!"

"NO!" Lila screamed as she saw the Skylane wavering and rocking nose down toward the treetops.

"No!" said a reporter from one of the choppers. "Something's gone wrong! The airplane is out of control! A gallant rescue effort could very well end in tragedy!"

Aboard Eight Yankee Tango, Jay stirred slightly, but remained unaware that directly out the windshield were mountains, rocks, and trees, coming closer, faster and faster.

SIX

Everybody keep your distance!" Ben Parker commanded through his headset. "Back off!"

The news choppers kept their distance but kept their cameras on the action. The Coast Guard chopper kept climbing to try and stabilize above the struggling Skylane.

"Give it time," said Brock, trying to reassure Dr. Cooper. "If that autopilot is still working and the control surfaces aren't bent, it might recover."

Even as they watched, Eight Yankee Tango dove downward until it gained enough speed to develop the lift necessary to pull it out of the dive, then nosed up into a climb. Then it climbed until it ran out of speed to maintain lift, nosed over into a dive again, then gained speed and lift and pulled up into a climb again, then slowed down and nosed down again, and so it went, like a roller coaster. Brock and Dr. Cooper got queasy just watching it.

Each successive dive was shallower and each

climb less steep. Eventually, it seemed the airplane might stabilize.

"About fifty minutes of fuel left," Dr. Cooper figured.

Brock called the tower, "Boeing Tower, this is Niner Zulu Mike. What's the word on that Coast Guard chopper? Are they going to try again?"

Ben Parker and Bob Konishi had just had a conference with Coast Guard Two Zero Bravo. Parker spoke into his headset. "Uh, negative, Niner Zulu Mike. The man who went out on the cable says it's just too risky. We would have lost the aircraft if he hadn't aborted."

Dr. Cooper could see The Yank still making shallow climbs and descents. He realized what the tower chief was saying was true. They'd come terribly close to losing both the plane and the Coast Guard's rescuers.

"So what's the plan now?" asked Dr. Cooper, fearful of the answer.

"The chopper's going to double back to pick up their man, and then they'll follow Yankee Tango until . . . whatever happens, happens," Parker replied.

Dr. Cooper looked at Brock, who muttered regretfully, "A ditch in the ocean, most likely."

"Dad . . . ?" came a faint voice over the other radio.

Dr. Cooper's heart skipped a beat. He was afraid to hope for too much as he switched radios and pressed his talk button. "Jay? Did you call?"

Jay was aware of his surroundings again, aware of the noisy cockpit and the stench of his own vomit and the sickening motions of the airplane. His head still hurt and he still couldn't see, but strangely enough, he felt stronger and more aware. "Dad? Hello?"

His father's voice was obviously excited. "Right here, Jay! How are you?"

Jay felt his forehead. The blood was drying. Apparently the bleeding had stopped. "Oh, not bad, considering."

"You've been out for a while."

"I feel like it. But I feel better. Maybe the nap did me some good."

Dr. Cooper felt Brock's joyous slap on his back as he replied, "That's great. Jay, you're out over the Olympic Peninsula heading for the ocean. How about a left turn on that autopilot to get you headed back toward Seattle?"

"I think I can handle that."

With jubilation, Brock and Dr. Cooper saw Eight Yankee Tango begin a gradual, steady left turn.

"And how about a touch of power," Cooper radioed. "You've lost a bit of altitude and we'd like to get you back up again."

"Okay. Adding some power."

"How's Rex?"

"Still out," came the answer.

A few cheers went up from the people gathered in the lounge as they saw Eight Yankee Tango turning back toward home, accompanied by Brock's Skylane, the news helicopters, and the lumbering Coast Guard Two Zero Bravo. They'd heard Jay's voice and were glad he was awake again, but they knew the danger wasn't over.

"What do you think they're going to do now?" one reporter asked another.

"Probably ditch it in Puget Sound," the other answered.

Lila didn't like the sound of that. "Ditch it?"

Johnny Adair was on hand to explain, "Just have him land in the water, then they come down with the chopper and some divers and pluck them out. Simple."

Lila studied the television images. "Why don't they just have Jay land it?"

Adair replied quietly, "That would be impossible. Your brother can't see."

But the idea stuck in her head, as ideas in Lila's head were often prone to do. She confided to her aunt, "I think he could land it."

A reporter wearing a headset addressed the camera from on-board chopper seven, the Olympic Mountains visible through the window behind her, the whine of the helicopter audible behind her voice. "Fourteen-year-old Jay Cooper, who has been unconscious, is again conscious and coherent. He's turned the airplane around, and now the airplane is heading back toward Seattle. According to a Boeing Tower spokesman, it is very likely the boy's father, acting as a seeing-eye pilot, will try to guide his son to an attempted water landing in Puget Sound."

Dr. Cooper and Brock were on the radio with the tower chief and a representative from the Coast Guard.

Dr. Cooper was feeling grim. "Okay," he said. "I'll see if he's up to that."

"He'll have to be," Ben Parker replied. "But you don't have to tell him everything."

"I understand." Dr. Cooper switched to the other radio tuned to the Auburn frequency, the one they'd been using to talk to Jay all this time. But he didn't call. He sat there, struggling within himself.

Brock offered, "You don't have to tell him."

"Yes I do," Dr. Cooper protested. "I know Jay. He's going to ask. It's going to matter to him, as well it should."

"So what are you going to tell him?"

"What I've always told him: the truth." He pressed his talk button. "Jay, as near as we can figure, you only have about forty to forty-five minutes of fuel left. Now, the Coast Guard tried to fly over and snag you with a cable, but that didn't work and we almost lost you. So the plan now is to get you back to the Sound, set up a safe descent rate, and land you in the water. The Coast Guard chopper will follow you and drop divers and life rafts to pull you out. Does that sound like a plan?"

Jay had plenty of questions, but for now said simply, "Okay."

"Now son . . . ," his father purposely spoke evenly, clearly. "You need to take a careful inventory of your abilities. I won't lie to you. When the plane hits the water, it'll be a rough landing. It might flip over and you'll be upside down. You're going to get wet, because the cabin is going to fill up with water. You're going to have to unbuckle yourself, get the door open, and swim out of there, and fast, because the airplane is going to sink. Do you have the strength to do that?"

Jay sat up straight and stretched a little. His arms were working, and so were his legs. He still couldn't see, but his mind felt surprisingly clear. "If God will help me, I think I can do it."

He could sense a warmth in his father's voice when Dr. Cooper said, "Well, God has certainly helped you up to this point. I believe we can trust Him for the rest."

Then Jay reached over and felt his uncle's limp hand. It was still warm, and there was still a pulse. "What about Uncle Rex?"

Dr. Cooper and Brock exchanged a look.

"Uh, we'll get to that, son. It'll be kind of tricky." There was a moment of dead air. "Uh, Jay?"

"He might die, huh?"

That question came abruptly. Dr. Cooper swallowed. The same question had been at the forefront of his mind since all this started, but he kept pushing it aside. Now Jay was bringing it right out in the open. "Son, this is a serious situation involving an overwhelming degree of risk. By God's grace you'll survive, but . . . yes, there's a good chance things won't work out the way we wish."

Jay came back, "Well, I just wanted you to know I was thinking about it. Sitting here in this airplane with no eyes, you start thinking about stuff like that."

"Yeah, that's for sure. I've been thinking about it too." Dr. Cooper searched his own heart for the faith he'd always taught his kids to have. It was still there, but he knew it was being challenged this day. "I guess we're in a real trust-God situation, aren't we?"

"Oh yeah. But He knows what's best. We just have to put ourselves in His hands and let Him take it where He wants to take it. Uncle Rex and I are ready, I know that."

Dr. Cooper felt close to tears. "I'm proud of you, son."

85

Jay couldn't believe what he was saying and how calm he felt about it all, and yet it was true. He was only fourteen, but he'd faced death and walked with God enough to know who was really in charge and who controlled the outcome of situations like this. As he told his Dad, sitting in this airplane without sight, it was only natural to confront the whole issue and get it settled.

"Well, I love you, Dad. Always have."

"And I love you too, son."

"Tell Lila I love her."

"You can tell her yourself. I'm sure she's listening to our radio transmissions."

"I love you, Lila."

In the tower lounge, Lila broke into tears. "I love you too, Jay." Suddenly, Johnny Adair reached through the crowd and handed Lila a handheld radio. She took it, swallowed back her tears, and spoke it again, "I love you, Jay."

"Hi, Sis!" he replied. The joy in his voice was obvious. "How you doing?"

"Oh, just great!" she replied. "Guess you'll be going swimming today."

"That's what I hear."

"We're all praying for you."

"Well . . . then I can't lose, can I? Is Aunt Joyce there?"

Lila handed the radio to Joyce, and Joyce said, "Hello, Jay. This is Aunt Joyce."

"Aunt Joyce." Jay's voice wavered with emotion as he told her, "We're going to be all right, both me and Uncle Rex. Don't you worry."

Joyce's eyes welled up with tears. "Just do your best, Jay. Land it gently, and we'll see you both real soon."

"See you."

Joyce was just about to hand the radio back to Adair when Dr. Cooper's voice came over the scanner. "Boeing Tower, can I speak to my sister on this frequency?"

"Stand by," they heard Ben Parker reply. "Adair, how about it?"

Adair realized Dr. Cooper was using the tower frequency, the one Jay would not be able to hear. He told Joyce, "Go ahead. It's 121.5, same as your scanner."

Joyce twisted in the new frequency. "Jake, this is Joyce."

Her brother's voice was gentle but grim. "We're in a bad situation, sis."

Joyce drew upon all the courage she had as she replied, "I understand."

"Somehow . . . if we can just get Rex to wake up—"

"Jacob," she said so strongly she was almost scolding, "I don't expect any miracles from you, you hear me? That's God's department. You and your son just do your best. Rex belongs to the Lord, and the Lord will take care of him."

Now Dr. Cooper's voice was choked with emotion. "We'll do our best. Talk to you soon."

"Godspeed, Jacob."

Joyce handed the radio back to Adair and then collapsed in tears.

"They'll be all right," Lila whispered as they embraced.

Dr. Cooper drew a deep breath and moved on to business. "Boeing Tower, where would you like us to ditch the plane?"

Ben Parker's voice came back, "Just off Alki Point would work. Close to shore. We'll have emergency vehicles on hand."

"Roger, Alki it is."

Dr. Cooper looked ahead and could see the sky-scrapers of Seattle on the horizon. In just a few minutes they would be over Puget Sound. "All right, Jay, two things we have to do: slow down and start a descent. We'll get the speed down first just like we did before."

Brock told Jay how much to throttle back, and they both trimmed their airplanes, then repeated. Time passed and Seattle drew closer as they went through the sticky, finicky process of getting both aircraft down to seventy knots—the airplane's recommended speed for approaching a landing. That was slow for a Skylane, and Brock could feel the sluggishness of his controls and the shaky, swervy feel of his slow-moving airplane.

Dr. Cooper studied the chart in his lap. "About

ten nautical miles to Alki from here . . . about eight and a half minutes."

Brock did some figuring in his head. "We'll have dropped seventeen hundred feet by the time we get there. We're at twenty-six hundred now. That'll do. Once we get there we'll have him circle down the remaining nine hundred."

Dr. Cooper radioed, "All right, Jay, we're headed for Alki. You need to get ready for ditching. Are there any loose objects in the airplane that could fly around and hurt you if the airplane flips?"

Jay sighed at the fact that he couldn't see to answer the question. "Probably. We had some cameras and stuff. I don't know what Uncle Rex has stowed in the luggage compartment."

"How about your coat?"

"I've got that on the backseat."

"See if you can reach back and grab that. You'll want to wrap it around your head right before landing to protect your face."

"Okay." He reached back with his left hand and felt his coat. He pulled that through the space between the front seats and set it in his lap. "Okay, got it."

"What about Rex? Is there anything to protect his head?"

"I think maybe I can reach his coat. Hang on." Jay reached back again and felt Rex's coat. He pulled that forward. "I've got his coat." There was no answer. "Hello?"

Dr. Cooper hesitated, then said quickly, "Okay, stand by, son." He spoke to Brock, "He'll try to get Rex out."

Brock nodded. "I know. An injured, weakened, and blind kid is going to try to pull a two-hundred-thirty-pound man from a sinking airplane that might be upside down. Jake, if it flips they'll be hanging upside down from their seat belts with their heads in the water. If Rex doesn't wake up—"

"Are you sure about the sink rate?"

Brock insisted, "You heard what Fleming and the tower guy said, and I agree. That plane will be so full of openings it'll flood with water in seconds. Jay won't have time to pull Rex out and save himself too. If he tries to pull Rex out, they'll both go down with the airplane."

"Dad?" Jay called on the radio. "Hello?"

Dr. Cooper put his finger on the talk button, but then asked Brock, "What if he tried to land the plane—on land?"

Brock scowled. "Don't be crazy! You'd lose them both. At least this way you have a good chance of saving your son!"

"Dad?" came Jay's voice again.

Dr. Cooper pressed the talk button. "Son, make sure the doors are unlatched. That way, even if the cabin gets bent up, you'll still be able to swing them open."

"Okay."

"And son, I'd make sure the windows are left open too. That way the water pressure won't keep you from getting the doors open."

"All right." Jay loosened his seat belt and reached across in front of his uncle to find the window latch on the left side. With a quick little twist the latch released and the window popped open, letting in a rush of wind. The door latch was large and easy to find. He flipped it up and the door unlatched. The wind held the door loosely shut, but came shrieking in through all the cracks around it.

"Left turn, Jay," came Brock's voice.

Jay found the autopilot turn knob and turned it to the left just the right amount. He could feel the airplane doing *something,* but had to trust it was a turn.

The latch for Jay's door was near his right hand and he found it easily, pulling it up and unlatching the door. It popped loose, letting more wind and noise into the cabin. By now the cockpit was a canful of noise: the fierce rush of the wind, the roar of the engine, the rattling and vibrating of the airframe. Jay was afraid he wouldn't be able to hear further instructions in his headset. "Okay. Doors are unlatched, windows are open. It's noisy in here. How's the turn going?"

"Looks good. Just keep it turning until I tell you to roll out."

"Okay."

Brock and Dr. Cooper followed Eight Yankee Tango as it made a slow, descending turn to the north over Puget Sound.

"Two thousand feet," Brock reported.

"And about five and a half minutes to Alki," Dr. Cooper figured.

"Okay, Jay, roll out."

The Skylane out their window rolled out of the turn and continued a straight descent.

Dr. Cooper was praying, struggling in his soul. *Come on, Rex. Come on!* He pressed the talk button. "Jay, how's Rex? Is he stirring at all?"

Jay reached over and nudged his uncle, but there was no response. "Uncle Rex?" He reached up and thumped his uncle's face with his fingers. No response.

"Give us another left turn, Jay," said Brock. "This will be a short one."

Jay found the knob and turned it. This time he could feel the plane lean to the left. "Dad, Uncle Rex is out cold. He's still breathing, but he must really be hurt bad."

"Stop the turn," Brock instructed, and Jay turned the knob to neutral.

"Jay, slap him," Dr. Cooper ordered desperately. "Yell at him. Pinch him, I don't care. He has to wake up."

Jay reached over, found his uncle's face, and gave it a slap. "Uncle Rex! Hello! Good morning! Come on, rise and shine, we've got a plane to land!"

There was no response.

Jay radioed back, "He's out, Dad. He could be dying for all I know."

Dr. Cooper dropped his head in despair, but he quickly forced himself to straighten up and gather a stern resolve. "Then let it go, son. Concentrate on flying the plane. Let's get you down."

He could see Alki Point approaching. It was a large, squarish section of Seattle jutting out into Puget Sound with a lighthouse on its northwest corner. A well-traveled, four-lane street ran along the shoreline, with bike and rollerblade rental shops, restaurants, boutiques, and rows of expensive homes packed shoulder to shoulder facing the view. Traffic would probably be heavy on that street today and on the public beach. It was going to be quite a show.

"Fifteen hundred feet," Brock reported.

Ben Parker's voice came through their headsets. "Winds are southeasterly at ten knots. I recommend you approach to the south along the west shoreline."

"South along the west shoreline," Brock acknowledged, then told Dr. Cooper, "We'll keep him heading north, then turn him around and bring him back south again. We'll time it so he hits the water just off the Point."

Dr. Cooper could see a white and red Coast Guard cruiser racing into position just off Alki Point. Another Coast Guard chopper was already hovering above the water, its rotor like a silver windmill in the sun.

He radioed, "Jay, we're almost abeam Alki, descending through twelve hundred feet. We're just a little high, but we'll keep heading north to bleed off some more altitude, then turn you around. I can see a Coast Guard boat and helicopter down there right now waiting for you."

"Okay," Jay answered.

"Better get Rex's coat over his head to protect him, and then get yourself wrapped up too."

"Okay. I've got his coat here. I'll put it over his head."

"Don't smother him."

"I won't."

"And then cover your own head. I'll let you know how high you are above the water so you can brace yourself."

As they waited for Jay to complete the task, a question just about leaped out of Dr. Cooper's mouth, "Jay, I'm just wondering, do you think you could—" He held it back.

"Say again?"

"Uh, nothing. How's Rex doing?"

"I've got his coat over his head but it's loose enough for him to breathe."

Brock joined in, "Okay, we're at nine hundred

feet. Jay, we're going to continue north for two minutes, then make a right turn back to the south, and then two minutes after that, you should land in the water."

"Make sure your seat belts are tight," Dr. Cooper advised.

"Roger. Seatbelts secure."

"Good." And now it was time to deal with the subject he'd been dreading. "Jay, listen to me now: the moment you hit the water. . . ." The words stuck in his throat. "The moment you hit the water, you need to get out of the airplane." That wasn't saying it. Dr. Cooper started digging in his heart and mind for the words.

"I'm not worried about me," Jay answered. "I'm just not sure if I can get Uncle Rex out."

Dr. Cooper made a fist in his pain and frustration, then forced the words out. "Son, the truth is, you can't. Listen to me. We've had several people consulting on this and they all agree that the plane won't stay afloat long enough for you to pull Rex out of there."

Jay felt a stab through his stomach. "I don't think I understand."

Brock's voice broke in, "Seven hundred feet and one minute to the turn, Jay. Stand by."

"Dad?"

His father spoke haltingly, painfully. "Son, once the airplane hits and starts filling up with water, you'll only have enough time to get yourself out. If you try to get Rex unbuckled and out the door before you get yourself out, you'll both go down with the plane. Do you understand?"

Joyce shook her head. Her whole body trembled. "No . . . NO!" Lila reached out to hold her. Some staff also came alongside to restrain her as Joyce started screaming. "NO! DEAR GOD, NO!"

Jay understood, but couldn't believe it. "You're . . . you're saying that Uncle Rex is going to drown?"

His father replied, "We don't know that for sure. Something else could happen we don't foresee. Maybe the divers will be able to get to the plane in time. We don't know. We only know that you won't have time to save him *and* yourself."

Jay actually felt angry. "Then why are we *doing* this?"

Dr. Cooper still had that unasked question burning in his heart. "Son, there's still one alternative, if you're willing."

Jay was already ahead of him. "Why don't we just go back to Boeing Field and *land* this thing on the ground?"

Brock shook his head, but Dr. Cooper was determined to settle the question. "Jay, are you sure about that?"

Brock interrupted, "Right turn, Jay. One hundred eighty degrees, about a minute long, start now."

Jay was still angry, and his mind was brewing up a storm as he tweaked the autopilot knob to the right and began the turn. "I'm sure I'm not going to leave my Uncle Rex to drown in a sinking airplane!"

Brock's voice cut in, "Jay, it's a choice I would recommend if you want to live. This is no time to be a hero."

Lila could bear it no more. Johnny Adair was busy helping the others restrain Joyce, who was still crying and wailing for Rex. His handheld radio lay on a table nearby. She grabbed it up, pressed the talk button, and said, "Jay, this is Lila! Go to Boeing Field! Land the plane!"

Adair groped at her, trying to grab his radio. "No! Don't tell him that!"

But Lila only jerked away from Adair and repeated it. "You hear me, Jay Cooper? Land the plane! You can do it!"

Brock shouted "No" to no one in particular, but Dr. Cooper felt his heart soar as they heard Lila continue, "God is with you, and He loves you, and He can guide your hands, I just know it! Nobody has to die today if God doesn't want it to happen! You can land it, Jay, I know you can!"

Brock spoke sternly, "Lila, get off the frequency. Jay, roll out of the turn! Four hundred feet. Prepare to ditch!"

As people gathering on the beach at Alki watched, pointing, peering through binoculars, the Skylane rolled out of the turn and came at them from the north, sinking lower and lower over the water. The Coast Guard chopper hovered above the lighthouse, watching and ready; the news choppers shadowed the airplane like big mosquitoes, the rumble of their rotors carrying loud and clear across the water.

Jay reached over and found his uncle's hand, still warm. He felt for his pulse, and quickly felt his chest and head. "You're counting on me, aren't you, Uncle Rex?"

Then in a decisive moment, he radioed, "Dad, what do you think?"

Brock cut in, "Don't be a fool!"

"Mr. Axley," Jay said angrily, "I'm asking my *father!*"

Brock snapped back, "Two hundred feet to touch down, Mr. Cooper! Get ready!"

They were chasing alongside Eight Yankee Tango as it descended, its shadow on the water drawing ever closer to its wheels.

Dr. Cooper only had a few seconds to think of an answer. It would be a choice between saving Jay's life and most likely losing them both, and yet, with a strange, unnatural peace, the answer came to him. He knew what his son would do, given the choice. "Jay, with Rex unable to pilot the aircraft, that makes you pilot-in-command. We can all tell you what we think, but only you can decide. I'm with you, son, one hundred percent."

There was no answer from Eight Yankee Tango. In the few seconds left before it would hit the water, Jay Cooper was thinking, praying.

"Thirty seconds to impact," said Brock Axley.

SEVEN

Jay had only a brief second to cry out to the Lord.
"It's all Yours," he said.
And then he shoved the throttle forward.
"Let's land it!" he yelled.
Only a few feet off the water, The Yank roared to life, nosed up, and climbed like a homesick angel.

Brock shoved his throttle forward and climbed after The Yank as he gave Dr. Cooper a troubled, bewildered look.

Dr. Cooper objected, "Hey, I didn't tell him what to do. It was his decision."

Brock scowled. "But you knew what he'd do!"

Dr. Cooper smiled proudly. "Yeah. I knew."

Brock stewed for a moment, and then just shook his head in amazement, if not admiration. "Okay, let's land it."

The people on the shore had mixed reactions as The Yank, followed by Zulu Mike, flew right by them, climbing together into the sky. Some moaned with disappointment; but those having heard the communications over their scanners began to cheer.

"It's not over yet," said the lady in Channel 7's chopper as the camera showed the two planes regaining altitude over the sound. "Having made a remarkable, courageous decision, young Jay Cooper will attempt to land the plane!"

Joyce and Lila embraced, not in joy, but in renewed hope. As the lady on the television said, it wasn't over yet.

The reporters in the room were shoving microphones in Johnny Adair's face.

"What do you think of this decision?"

"What are his chances of a successful landing?"

"What happens now?"

Adair just looked toward the ceiling, thinking of the folks upstairs in the control room. "Parker's gonna love this."

Ben Parker had not been idle. The moment he heard Jay say he was going to land the Skylane he had turned to Bob Konishi. "Bob, tell the Coast Guard boys to stay right where they are. We'll still need them . . . if this doesn't work out." He told Josie Fleming, "And let's get the fire trucks and emergency vehicles out on the field."

Konishi got on the radio; Fleming got on the phone. Across the field, the fire trucks appeared from their garage, their lights flashing.

In the control room, all eyes were now on Ben Parker. He was standing in the middle of the room, his hands on his hips, his grim, brooding face like chiseled granite. They could tell his steely gaze was not focused on the runways visible through the window but on the mental image of that Skylane.

Abruptly, he went to his console, switched frequencies, and spoke into his headset, "November Seven Five Eight Yankee Tango, Boeing Tower."

Jay realized at once that the Boeing control tower was calling him. "Boeing Tower, Skylane Seven Five Eight Yankee Tango, go ahead."

"We understand you are now pilot-in-command of the aircraft. What are your intentions, sir?"

Jay felt honored to be so addressed but didn't let it go to his head. Instead, he set his jaw and his determination and replied, "Eight Yankee Tango requests a landing at Boeing Field, full stop."

Dr. Cooper listened, smiling from deep inside and nodding in approval.

Ben Parker checked the weather console and replied, "Roger, Eight Yankee Tango, you are clear for landing straight in on Runway One Three Right. Winds are One Six Zero at Eight." The wind was coming from 160 degrees on the compass, or from the southeast, at a speed of eight knots. "The altimeter . . ." he almost smiled in amusement. "Well, for all of you up there who can see, current altimeter is Three Zero One Five."

Brock adjusted the altimeter in his airplane to the correct barometric pressure Ben Parker had given and then turned to Dr. Cooper. "Take him in, Jake. I'm with you."

Dr. Cooper radioed, "Jay, we're up to one thousand. Ease back the power about one finger's length and start a right turn."

"Roger," said Jay. "Pulling back the power, and here goes a right turn."

They followed The Yank as it climbed through a wide, gentle turn to the right.

"We're going to take you up north," said Dr. Cooper, "and then turn you around and line you up with the runway to bring you straight in. Boeing Tower, did you copy?"

Ben Parker replied, "Roger, Zulu Mike, we copy." He stole a glance at Barbara Maxwell, who was searching her radar screen and talking to any other aircraft in the area. "We are advising other traffic to leave the area. The sky's all yours."

"Interesting day," Parker observed to Maxwell, who nodded.

"Okay," said Dr. Cooper. "One more half a finger joint out on that throttle and you should be about there."

Brock and Dr. Cooper watched carefully as The Yank's nose eased down and the airplane began to level out of the climb. The two Skylanes, accompanied by the three news helicopters, were at fifteen hundred feet—the blue waters of Puget Sound below them, the impressive Seattle skyline off to their right. They were heading north toward a point of land commonly called West Point, a peninsula that jutted into the Sound and had the distinction of being Seattle's westernmost piece of real estate. From there, an aviator could look southeast and see right down Runway One Three Right at Boeing Field, about nine miles away.

"Winds one six zero," Brock mused. "That means he's going to have a thirty degree crosswind coming from his right. He's going to drift sideways over that runway."

"How wide is the runway?" Dr. Cooper asked.

"Two hundred feet, I think. And ten thousand feet long."

"Looks like we'll have a little bit of room—if the wind doesn't kick up any worse."

"Well, he doesn't have to use a runway, I suppose," Brock considered out loud. "Just as long as he lands somewhere that's flat and doesn't hit any people or runway lights or signs or vehicles or parked airplanes or buildings."

"We're not asking for much, are we?"

They reached West Point and all five aircraft made a slow, steady turn like a flock of birds to the southeast. Brock maneuvered Zulu Mike to a position slightly above and behind Yankee Tango. From there, Dr. Cooper had a good view of The Yank and what it was doing. Five miles away was the south shore of Elliot Bay, prickly with wharves, shipyards, and warehouses. Beyond that lay the wide, flat Duwamish Valley covered with low-structured factories, warehouses, freeways, and overpasses. Beyond that, nine miles in the distance, Runway One Three Right lay like a big gray stripe on a field of smog-hazed green.

Jay closed his eyes to pray out of habit, but again, it made little difference in what he could see. He prayed along as he heard his father pray, "Dear

Lord, Rex and Jay are in Your hands. We ask You for Your mercy and protection, and we trust You for the outcome. We love You, Lord, no matter what. Amen."

"Amen."

"Amen," said Ben Parker and all his crew.

As soon as Joyce and Lila said "Amen" and opened their eyes, they were on their feet.

"We've got to get out there!" said Joyce.

"Please, get us out there!" Lila told Johnny Adair.

Adair nodded and then led a parade—Joyce, Lila, and about twenty television and newspaper reporters with notepads, mikes, and cameras—out into the hall to the elevators and then down to the street level. A security fence stood between them and the vast apron where light planes, cargo planes, and commercial airliners were all parked. Beyond all those parked airplanes was Runway One Three Right.

While the reporters and camera people spread out along the fence looking for the best possible view through all the parked aircraft, Johnny Adair led Joyce and Lila to a gate, punched in a security code, and led them through. In a moment, they stood with nothing between them and the runway but a wide field of grass.

Traffic on the West Seattle Freeway was coming to a standstill as motorists, informed by their car radios, stopped to see the spectacle: two nearly identical Skylane aircraft flying in formation, followed by three news helicopters, all moving slowly over the bay and then right overhead, the airplane engines droning, the chopper blades wop-wop-wopping, heading for Boeing Field to the south. Horns began to honk, people waved, and a paint salesman leaned out the window of his van and hollered, "Godspeed, Jay Cooper!"

As Joyce and Lila continued to watch through binoculars, the two Skylanes grew to a clear and discernible shape; even their markings were recognizable: Eight Yankee Tango, white with red stripes, flying on the lower left of their view, and Niner Zulu Mike, white with green stripes, flying on the upper right.

The image blurred as tears filled Lila's eyes. She wiped them clear and kept watching.

"I can't take this, " Joyce moaned. "I don't think I can take this." Nevertheless, she remained standing where she was, solid as a post, peering through her binoculars. "Come on, Jay. Come on. I love that big guy!"

Dr. Cooper could see the runway getting closer, and his heart was pounding so hard he could feel it. "All right, Jay, descent power again. We'll start down."

"Okay, descent power."

"Four miles," said Brock. "Nine hundred feet. We might need a steeper descent rate before long."

Dr. Cooper instructed Jay, "Remember now, right before touchdown you'll probably have to pull off the power and raise the nose, but you have to do it slowly, gently. You've landed our plane before, you know how it feels."

Jay could feel his heart beginning to race. His hands were beginning to shake a little despite his efforts to steady them. "I know how it feels . . . I'll try to remember." He reached out and took hold of the control yoke. It felt familiar in his hands, but he dared not tug or push on it, not yet. *Oh Lord, help me to remember, help me to feel it.*

There was no sensation quite like being blind in a hurtling piece of flying machinery, having no real sense of where you were or where you were going or what might be in front of you. Jay tried to imagine what it was like outside the windows as he asked, "Where are we?"

"Three and half miles from the runway," said his father. "The I-5 freeway is off to your left, the Duwamish River is off to your right. You're about eight hundred feet up. It's a sunny day so far. I can see the numbers on the end of the runway, a big one three. Give me a touch of right."

Now Ben Parker and his crew were all watching through binoculars, looking out the huge windows of the control tower.

"We have you in sight, Yankee Tango," said Parker. "You look good so far. Winds one seven zero.

"Two mile final," said Brock. "Five hundred feet. Lots of room, just hold her steady."

Dr. Cooper peered through the windshield. Runway One Three Right was almost two miles long, and yet from up here it looked so small, so narrow, like a little sidewalk with a strip of green grass on either side. Outside the strip of grass on the right were a taxiway, huge 747s and 757s parked in a long row, light aircraft, a huge hanger. Straight down, the buildings, streets and houses of Georgetown were passing rapidly under them, getting bigger and closer and faster with each passing second.

The two airplanes passed over the north airport boundary and their shadows appeared on the grass just north of the runway threshold. The broad, white-striped end of One Three spread out before them, coming up fast.

Yankee Tango veered to the right.

"Touch left," said Cooper.

Jay twisted the autopilot knob to the left, waited just a moment, then returned it to neutral.

"Touch right," came his father's voice again.

He twisted the knob to the right. The airplane hit a bump in the air and lurched. Jay's hand fell from the knob. He groped to find it again. Precious time passed.

The Yank banked over into a steep right turn.

Dr. Cooper tried to keep his voice calm, but his words shot out with rapid-fire urgency. "You're turning right, Jay! Back to neutral, back to neutral!"

Jay groped for the knob with his left hand, grabbed the yoke with his right. He turned the yoke to the left momentarily, trying to override the autopilot.

"No . . . no, straighten it out!" Lila cried as she watched Yankee Tango pass over the runway and then beyond it, rocking this way, then that, caught in ground turbulence.

Jay found the knob and twisted it back to neutral.

The Yank snapped out of the turn, but now the airplane was fifty feet off the ground, still sinking, and headed for a row of 747s parked to the right of the runway.

This landing was too far gone to save.

"Full throttle, Jay," said Dr. Cooper. "Go around."

With a grimace of disappointment, Jay jammed the throttle forward and felt pressed into his seat as the airplane roared and rattled to life.

Through the telephoto lens of a television camera on the field, the Skylane appeared to drop behind the monstrous tail fin of a 747—as if it was sure to collide with it.

Then, like a barn swallow in a graceful upswoop, it shot up from behind the tail fin and into the sky, nose high, wings level.

Audiences all over the Northwest could hear a sigh of relief from the reporter and his cameraman.

Ben Parker let his head droop for just a moment of quiet relief, then looked out the window again as the Skylane climbed toward them. "Keep climbing, baby, keep climbing."

If the Skylane did not continue climbing, it would certainly fly right through the tower windows.

Trust, trust, TRUST! Jay kept telling himself as he forced himself to hold still, keep his hands off the yoke, and not panic as he waited for the next word of instruction from his father.

Dr. Cooper managed to keep his voice so calm he surprised even himself as he said, "Okay, Jay, now let's give it a touch of left so you don't run into the control tower."

The Skylane made a neat, brief bank to the left. "Perfect."

Jay's voice came back. "Dad, I'm sorry. My hand slipped off the knob."

Dr. Cooper drew a deep breath. He didn't want his voice to sound unsteady as he replied, "That's okay, son. You did great. We're going to go around and try it again."

Just then, Ben Parker's voice came over the other radio, the one Jay would not hear. "Niner Zulu Mike, call me on this frequency."

Brock switched radios. "Niner Zulu Mike here."

Ben Parker spoke through his headset as he and his crew watched Eight Yankee Tango fly by the tower, safely to one side. "Be advised that by our best figures, Eight Yankee Tango has enough fuel for only one more attempted landing. Do you copy?"

Brock shot a glance at Dr. Cooper, then replied, "Roger, we copy."

Parker's face was stony and grim, his voice even. "If the aircraft runs out of fuel over a populated area, some innocent people on the ground could be hurt or killed. I'm sure you understand that."

Brock looked at Dr. Cooper, who nodded.
Brock replied, "Roger, we understand."
"If this attempt fails, you are instructed to guide the aircraft back to Alki Point where the Coast Guard is standing by. You are to follow through with the previous plan to ditch. Please acknowledge."
Reluctantly, Brock pressed his talk button. "We

acknowledge. If this attempt fails, we ditch the aircraft."

Dr. Cooper looked at Brock, and then out the window at Eight Yankee Tango, still climbing. "One more attempt. Let's make it good."

EIGHT

The flying armada climbed to one thousand feet, leveled off, turned to the north, and flew out over Puget Sound once again. For want of fuel—and out of fear for Jay's dwindling strength—they decided against going clear to West Point. They turned inbound over Elliot Bay, seven miles out, holding steady at one thousand feet. Brock and Dr. Cooper did not tell Jay this would be his last attempt; he had enough on his mind.

Dr. Cooper tried to keep his voice strong and even. He didn't want to pass any fear on to his son. "It looked good, Jay, it really did."

Jay was feeling tired and starting to get sick again, but more than that, a creeping terror was sneaking into his soul, giving him a gnawing pain in his gut and making his hands tremble. "What happened last time? It felt real bumpy."

His father explained, "We think it was turbulence coming around that big hangar. We're going to keep you up higher this time and land you farther down the runway. It's a trade-off. We won't have as much runway to play with, but hopefully the wind will be a little more steady and you won't get knocked around quite so much."

"I just . . . ," Jay's emotions were getting raw. "I just want to get on the ground again, that's all. I want to get out of this airplane! I want to use my eyes and walk with my own feet on solid ground!"

"I want the same thing for you, son." Dr. Cooper spoke soothingly. "As a matter of fact, we were all supposed to go down to the waterfront tonight, remember? We were going to get fish and chips and share it with the seagulls, then walk through the aquarium. Does that sound good to you?"

His father had mentioned the right things. It warmed Jay's heart just to think of them. "I'd love it."

"So what do you say? Let's get this plane on the ground and go home."

Jay drew a breath and sighed loudly as he let it out. Now he began gathering whatever strength and resolve he had left. "Let's do it."

"Right turn."

Jay twisted the knob for what seemed like the zillionth time. "Right turn."

A few seconds passed, and then his father said, "Stop turn."

Jay repeated, "Stop turn," and returned the knob to neutral.

And then he sat there, isolated from the world in a tight aluminum cocoon that to him had no windows. He was in the dark, surrounded by noise and rushing wind.

"Now when you're about to touch down, have one hand on the yoke and one hand on the throttle. You'll have to pull the power back when I tell you, and then you'll have to hold the nose up. It'll be tricky. But hey, if we can get you within a few feet of the runway, a few bumps aren't going to hurt anybody."

His father sounded so calm about all this, as if he'd done it every day of his life! *I wish I could see, Dad, like you.*

Dr. Cooper's eyes were riveted on the airplane carrying his son and brother-in-law. "Just a few more minutes. Just a few more—"

Brock checked the instruments. "Descending two hundred feet a minute. That'll do for now, but let's keep him up high enough to get past that stupid hangar."

The fire trucks motored further down the runway, having gotten word from Josie Fleming that the airplane would attempt a longer landing.

Out by Alki Point, the Coast Guard chopper and cruiser stood ready, listening to their radios, waiting for word.

Aboard the news helicopters, the reporters were so engrossed in the unfolding event that they said very little. They, as well as everyone watching their broadcast, could hear the painstaking, step-by-step radio communications between Dr. Cooper and his son. That and the image of the two airplanes descending together said it all.

"Looking good," said Brock. "Two mile final, five hundred."

Again, Runway One Three lay waiting for them, coming up fast. The buildings and streets of Georgetown seemed to move rapidly under and behind them. They were sinking, sinking, lower and lower.

"We're too low," said Brock. "More throttle."

"More throttle, Jay," ordered Dr. Cooper.

The cameras on the ground now began taping the two Skylanes approaching over the tops of the buildings, and the reporters by the fence picked up their narration:

"This could be it, *the* final moment."

"As all the world watches with held breath. . . ."

"Never in all my career have I witnessed a moment like this one."

Jay moved his hand from the throttle to the autopilot knob, then back to the throttle, then back to the autopilot knob, then back to the throttle, memorizing where they were. He could feel a little bit of stirring in the airframe, as if Yankee Tango were coming into some turbulence again. He reached for the yoke with his right hand and found it. He could feel the autopilot tweaking the yoke left, then right, then right again, then left, fighting the wind gusts, trying to keep the wings level.

"One mile, three hundred."

The two aircraft came over the north fence. Their shadows raced once more across the grass, coming closer, closer.

"Touch right," said Dr. Cooper, and this time his voice cracked. He cleared his throat and instructed again, "Touch right."

The Yank banked to the right then returned to neutral. They were coming in crooked, a little to the left of Runway One Three, their noses turned slightly to the right, into the wind. Dr. Cooper was trying to anticipate the wind, hoping to get The Yank over the runway.

They passed over the runway threshold. The big white numbers, one three, passed under them, only slightly to their right. Now they were using up the runway, losing hundreds of feet of it each moment.

"Hold her right there, Jay, steady as she goes. One hundred feet."

The shadow of Eight Yankee Tango was racing along the concrete of Runway One Three.

Jay reached down and gave his seat belt one last tightening tug, then placed his right hand on the yoke. This time he held the autopilot knob with his left thumb and index finger and braced his hand against the panel with his other fingers. He could not let his hand be jerked away from that knob again!

Brock eyed the end of the runway coming up fast. "Too much power, too much power, he won't get down in time!"

"Less power, Jay!" Dr. Cooper almost shouted. "Back it off easy."

Oh man, here goes. Jay cringed and prayed as he pulled the throttle back.

The Yank nosed down and began to drop faster toward its shadow on the pavement below.

Joyce let out one little cry and then ran for the fence. "I can't watch this, I can't watch!"

Johnny Adair opened his arms and held her as she buried her face in his chest.

Lila kept watching, no longer aware of the asphalt under her feet. In her mind and soul, she was in that airplane with her brother, feeling it, flying it, *willing* it to land on the runway.

"Come on now, easy, easy . . . ," she coached.

The two airplanes descended together, one over the runway, one over the grass. They were like twins, mirror reflections of each other. At fifty feet off the ground, Brock lowered ten degrees of flaps and throttled for level flight, keeping pace with the descending Yank.

"Hand on the throttle, Jay," said Dr. Cooper. "You're fifty feet off the runway."

Jay's hand was already there. He waited, knowing nothing but what his father told him. *Trust, Jay! Trust, trust, TRUST!*

"Forty feet. Don't pull the yoke yet. Relax. Remember, don't overcorrect."

The Yank's shadow moved to the left and over the grass.

"He's going to miss the runway!" Brock warned.

"Touch right."

The Yank banked to the right and now its shadow skittered along the runway's edge. They could feel the stirring, the lurching of turbulence close to the ground.

The shadow drifted to the left again.

"Touch right. Twenty feet."

The Yank banked right again. Half the shadow came over the runway.

They'd used up half the runway. Up ahead, the fire trucks and aid cars were waiting on the grass, lights flashing, medics and firefighters standing ready.

The shadow drifted left and off the runway.

"We won't make the runway," said Dr. Cooper.

"Let him finish it," Brock yelled. "Let him touch down."

"Ten feet," said Dr. Cooper. "Hand on that yoke, stand by!"

Jay could feel The Yank rocking, swaying, wagging its tail in small gusts of wind. His hands were shaking, trembling against the yoke and throttle. "Dear God, dear God, dear God. . . ."

"Start pulling the power back, Jay, *slowly!*"

"Oh God, oh God. . . ." He pulled. It seemed slow, but he couldn't be sure. The engine began to hush.

"Back pressure, Jay, just a touch."

He pulled on the yoke.

"Hold it there, hold it there!" Now his Dad was quite excited, his voice racing and high-pitched. "Five feet, hold it steady!"

The Yank was off to the left of the runway, heading for the grass. Brock looked anxiously ahead. Were there any lights, any signs, any obstacles?

A fire truck! A big stupid fire truck was sitting on the grass! The crew was scrambling, trying to move it. It was beginning to move, but—

CRUNCH!! RATTLE! The impact of the wheels on the ground came so suddenly, so loudly, that Jay's whole body jerked with a start.

Then the wheels were quiet. Jay felt like he was floating.

The Yank had bounced high. It was nose up, losing speed, heading for the fire truck.

"POWER, JAY!" Dr. Cooper yelled. "POWER!"

Jay jammed the throttle forward. The plane lurched, roared, rattled. Through the blur and blindness he thought he saw a flash of red.

As Lila watched, as the television cameras recorded it, as the crowds along the aprons and fences all watched in horror, Eight Yankee Tango pulled, struggled, clawed its way into the air, up ten feet, then fifteen, just enough to skim over the top of the red fire truck.

"Chop the power!" Dr. Cooper yelled. "Ease off the pressure!"

Jay yanked the throttle back so hard his hand slipped off the knob and his elbow slammed into his seat back. He could hear the engine flutter down to a whispering idle. At the same time he felt a sickening, sinking feeling like an elevator going down.

The Yank nosed down toward the grass, limping, floating through the air.

The stall horn began to wail through the cabin, warning Jay of slow speed, loss of lift, an impending disaster.

"Nose up!" came his father's voice.

Nose up? I'm about to stall this thing!

Faith. There was nothing else available.

He pulled back.

The Yank nosed up just as it hit the grass again, bounced, floated, bounced again.

Jay froze in his seat, waiting, just waiting, afraid to move anything, just waiting for the wheels to touch again.

THUMP! The wheels hit ground again. Jay winced, waiting, expecting another bounce, another terrible floating.

But then . . . at long last, there followed a blessed rumble and rattle and bouncing and shaking.

The Yank was *on the ground!* It was rolling along the ground!

As Brock's airplane flew past, Dr. Cooper turned in his seat and looked out the back window. "I can't see him! I can't see him!"

First the fire crew ran after The Yank, then all the emergency trucks and cars gave chase. Laboriously, The Yank rumbled along the grassy strip alongside the runway, clattered and banged

127

and bumped over a runway light, bounced across a taxiway. . . .

Jay finally thought of the brakes and jammed on them hard.

November Seven Five Eight Yankee Tango locked its wheels, dug out two long ruts in the grass, and finally came to a stop.

Lila exploded with a scream of joy and relief, leaping so high in the air she thought she'd never touch down again.

"He made it! He made it!"

She ran to Joyce and yanked her loose from her death grip on Johnny Adair, forcing her to look and believe it. "They made it! They landed!"

No power on earth could contain the roar from the crowds along the fence. Nothing could restrain their shouts, their leaps, their waving arms.

In the control tower there was total bedlam as every member of the staff shouted and waved through the big glass windows at the aircraft resting out there on the grass beside the runway. Even Ben Parker, at long last, broke into a smile, and raised his hands in the air in triumph.

In homes, restaurants, department stores, and everywhere else there was a television or radio, crowds of people cheered, embraced, and cried. The reporters on the scene were crying and shouting into their microphones so loudly they could not be understood.

Brock climbed for safe altitude and circled back over the field for a look. When Dr. Cooper finally saw The Yank sitting on the grass in one piece, now surrounded by fire trucks and rescue personnel, he flopped back in his seat, removed his headset, and let himself breathe again. Brock extended his hand, and Dr. Cooper grasped it firmly and gave it a shake. Neither had to say a word.

Jay felt weary and faint. Absentmindedly, out of habit, out of repeated training from his father, he reached for the mixture control and pulled it all the way back.

With no more fuel coming through its carburetor, the faithful engine finally rested, its black propeller spinning to a stop.

It was the last thing Jay remembered doing in the cockpit of Eight Yankee Tango before he came to the end of his strength and everything went black.

It isn't over. I'm still in the airplane. I'm still fly-ing, still blind. . . .

Jay awoke with a start.

"Whoa, it's okay," came his father's voice.

He looked around. He was in a hospital bed.

"How are you feeling?" asked Lila.

He gripped the sides of the bed. He was still feel-ing the weird sensation of being in the airplane, even though he could see the bed was sitting solidly on the floor.

Wait. He could *see* the bed? His eyes grew wide. He blinked.

He could see again! He could see the hospital room with its white curtains and clean white walls; the sunlight coming in the window; his father, sister, and Aunt Joyce standing by the bed.

"Wow," was all he could say.

"How do things look, son?" Dr. Cooper asked.

"They look great! *Man*, do they look great!"

Dr. Cooper raised his hand for a high five, and Jay reached and gave his palm a slap. Lila leaned over the bed and gave Jay a joyful hug.

"Am I okay?" he asked.

"You're going to be fine," Dr. Cooper answered. "The doctors had to operate to relieve the pressure on your brain. Looks like they succeeded."

Jay's hand went to his head and felt the bandages. "What about Uncle Rex?"

Aunt Joyce answered, "Well, he's—"

A voice came through the door. "He's still alive

130

and kicking, that's what he is!" It was Rex, sitting in a wheelchair, pushed along by a nurse. His head was all bandaged, but he was smiling and still had that mischievous glint in his eye. "He's got a lovely wife, a great bunch of in-laws, a slightly bent airplane that made it back, and a very good God, and he's thankful." With the nurse's help he rolled up alongside Jay's bed and extended his hand. "You saved our lives, buddy. You're one crack pilot."

When the Coopers and Kramers finally made it to the Seattle waterfront a week later, Jay was so absorbed in seeing everything—the sun on the water, the seaweed and barnacles on the pilings, the smooth, effortless soaring of the seagulls—that the rest of the group had to keep waiting for him while he lagged behind to look at it all, study it, and see it as he had never seen it before.

"You know," Jay said, looking out across the water, "I was ready to leave it all and go home to be with the Lord, but I'm still kind of glad the Lord said, 'Not yet'."

"I guess He still has some things for you to do down here," Dr. Cooper said with a smile.

Rex nodded. "I wouldn't mind a few more years with Joyce; I really wouldn't." Then he smiled that same teasing smile. "And besides that, one of these days I'll get to see you finally get your pilot's license." Then he looked concerned. "Uh, that is, if you haven't had the idea scared out of you by now."

People dining at a nearby seafood bar were sharing their meals with the seagulls, tossing bits of fish and French fries high into the air where the gulls would catch them in mid-flight. Jay was fascinated.

"Boy, nothing can fly like a seagull, you know that?"

Rex thought it over and responded, "Eh, I've come close."

Jay didn't take his eyes off a snow white seagull as it swooped down in a wide, graceful circle to intercept a thrown French fry. "So will I."

"God willing," said Dr. Cooper.

"God willing," Jay and Rex said together.

The Cooper Kids Adventure Series®

by Frank E. Peretti

Now that you've read *Flying Blind,* the eighth book in the Cooper Kids Adventure Series®, you won't want to miss any of the exciting books in this fiction series by master storyteller Frank E. Peretti. Each volume tells a story about the challenges faced by biblical archaeologist Dr. Jacob Cooper and his children, Jay and Lila, as they travel the world together.

Books 1–4 in the Cooper Kids Adventure Series® are available from Crossway Books. Books 5–8 are available from Tommy Nelson™, a division of Thomas Nelson, Inc.

Turn the page for a sneak-peek at the other adventures that await you in The Cooper Kids Adventure Series®!

Book 7—The Legend of Annie Murphy

In 1885, Cyrus Murphy struck gold in his Bodine, Arizona mine. According to town legend, his wife, Annie Murphy, murdered him out of greed. Just before she was to be hanged for the murder, she made a run for freedom and was shot trying to escape. Now, more than a hundred years later, some people in Bodine have reported seeing Annie Murphy's "ghost." The Coopers interrupt their vacation to investigate the stories and stumble across a truth that is even stranger than they could have guessed. The Coopers unwittingly become involved in a mystery that spans a century, finding themselves caught up in a puzzle whose solution lies hidden somewhere between the past and the present.

Book 6—The Deadly Curse of Toco-Rey

Lila and Jay Cooper have joined their dad on a mission to the jungles of Central America, where a group of American treasure hunters have already become the victims of the deadly curse of Toco-Rey. How did these explorers really meet their end? In their search for answers, the Coopers come face to face with the many dangers that the jungle holds—natives armed with deadly darts, traps set by an ancient civilization, and swarms of poisonous flying slugs. Before Dr. Cooper can solve the mystery, his children are kidnapped and his integrity is put to the test. What price will he pay to get his children back? Is the treasure in the burial tomb of Kachi-Tochetin really worth more than gold?

Book 5—The Secret of the Desert Stone

Biblical archeologist Dr. Jacob Cooper and his children, Jay and Lila, arrive in the African country of Togwana with one goal—to discover the secret behind the two-mile-high Stone that has mysteriously appeared overnight. Who could have excavated, carved, and transported such a colossal Stone without leaving any evidence of their work? What does the Stone mean? Is it the evil omen that many of the people of Togwana believe it to be? The Coopers' uneasiness soon turns into dread as they realize they are being kept in the watchful eye of the country's new government and its brutal dictator, Idi Nkromo. Nkromo wants the Stone removed and will not tolerate failure. Will the Coopers get to the bottom of the mystery that has put their very lives in danger? The answers to their many questions may come in unexpected places.

Book 4—Trapped at the Bottom of the Sea

Returning early from one of her father's expeditions, Lila Cooper is aboard an Air Force plane that is hijacked. Now she is a prisoner in a top-secret weapons pod—trapped at the bottom of the sea with no escape. Meanwhile, Lila's father, Dr. Cooper; her brother, Jay; and daring journalist Meaghan Flaherty travel to a remote corner of the Pacific in search of the missing plane. With a cannibal tribe ahead of them and a band of angry terrorists in hot pursuit, can they reach Lila before it's too late?

Book 3—The Tombs of Anak

When Jay and Lila Cooper and their archaeologist father enter the tombs of Anak, they hope to find Dr. Cooper's missing co-worker. Instead, they stumble onto a frightening religion and new mysteries that soon plunge them all into incredible danger. Who or what is Ha-Raphah? Why do the local villagers fear him? Will the Coopers understand the truth in time to avoid disaster, or will they be swept away by Ha-Raphah's desperate last attempt to preserve his evil powers?

Book 2—Escape from the Island of Aquarius

Odd things are happening on the exotic South Pacific island of Aquarius—and those things are raising some unusual questions. Could the tyrannical leader of the island colony be the missing person Dr. Jacob Cooper has been sent to find? If so, why is he acting so strangely? Deadly perils lie in store for the Coopers as they seek to solve the mystery. The only hope for Jay, Lila, and their father is to find a way to overcome the evil that holds the colonists in its grip before the entire island disintegrates.

Book 1—The Door in the Dragon's Throat

Making their way through a dark and mysterious cavern, Jay and Lila Cooper can't help wondering what really lies behind the Door in the Dragon's Throat—riches from a lost kingdom . . . or an ancient evil? As they seek to unlock the truth about the sinister legends, they find comfort in the certainty that God has protected them from danger many times before. But will Jay and Lila be able to conquer the force that lurks behind the Door in the Dragon's Throat?